Princess Mandy and Her Watchman

A Fake Marriage Bodyguard Romance

by Rada Lyubomirova

***

Neurodivergent Version

***

Alpha Eureka Edukasia, Inc., 2023.

First published on October 8th '2023.

Digital Version ISBN: **978-1-963038-58-3**

Paperback Print ISBN: **979-8-9884575-4-1**

Hardcover Print ISBN: **978-1-963038-38-5**

Travel Version ISBN: **978-1-963038-02-6**

Neurodivergent Version ISBN: **978-1-963038-12-5**

***

Alpha Eureka Edukasia, Inc., DE, USA.

https://www.compendiapublishing.com

FAIR WARNING

This publication contains explicit language, explicit romantic scenes, and unnatural mortality. Readers' discretion is advised.

This work of fiction is NOT suitable for minors. The age limits may vary from one area of jurisdiction to another.

In the absence of clear guidance and/or limitations from the governing bodies, the publisher and the author suggest that 21 years of age be the minimum age for reading this publication.

DISCLAIMER

This book series is a work of fiction that draws inspiration from a Southeast Asian folktale and history, with some parts added for a dramatic purpose.

This work of fiction is for entertainment purposes only and is NOT to be treated as a matter of fact or as the ground for theories. However, the publishing company and author support the continuation of education and learning. This publication may be treated as a subject to study in the language arts, literature, culture, psychology, or any other related department or faculty.

The manuscript and cover art of this literary work are not generated by artificial intelligence and may NOT be utilised for AI training without the written permission of the copyright owner.

Also by Rada Lyubomirova

To understand who the Great One and his wife are,
kindly read the **"LILITH AND SAMAEL"** book series.
Book 1—A Story of the Twin Flame
Book 2—The House of Alchemists
Book 3—The Guardian Prince of Rome

***

SLAVA DEITY

Lord of the Underworld: A Paranormal Shifter
Romance of Veles
Springtime Birth and Wintertime Rebirth:
A Psychic Paranormal Romance of Yarilo and Morana

MAX SAINT

A Fictional Biography
Growing Her Wings: A Romantic Novel for Aspiring
Pilots
Sky Flower: Romantic Stories of the Ones Who Were
Left Behind
Princess Mandy and Her Watchman: A Fake
Marriage Bodyguard Romance
Soul Contract: When Soulmates Became Twin Flame
Starseeds: The Twin Flame Reunion

***

THE ARK OF THE SHADOW-WORKERS:

Legend, Myth, and Folklore Retelling
A Sailing Legacy: Adventures of the Sea Captain
Princess Mandy and Her Watchman: A Fake
Marriage Bodyguard Romance
The Watchman of Salt and Dust: Svyatoslav Bratva
Romance
Firebird: A Second Chance Romance of the
Pilot-in-Command
House of the Sailors: Pirates of the North

Dedication

To the princesses and princes who feel the temptation of running towards the cliff to fly off without wings, remember that you still have a chance to abort the takeoff; remember that you always have a choice to keep your feet on the ground; keep looking forward to where the future holds; ...; ...; ...

Prologue One
Kolya

Around A Decade Ago

***

He handed me a letter, which I assumed was from his past life. A life that he needed to burn in the fire he was igniting.

   Those arks and metal birds are tools for the dust to be in command of.
   The sky, the constellations, and the wind speak to us, deck crews.
   Especially when it is time for us to make life-or-death split-second decisions.

   They are the handiwork of the Guardian.
   They are for us to seek Guidance.
   Not for the dust to control them.
   When the handiworks are on the move, they are for the dust to watch and listen to.

x

Once one little flower falls, she will not be among the dust.

The little flower will become the sky flower to fly higher.

She will be surrounding you.

Within the air you breathe in, moving the oxygen in the blood for you to keep going forward.

Within the atmosphere, armouring your flesh with protection.

Within the wind, whispering Guidance whenever you are in command of the artillery.

Within the whispers, the wisdom will be relayed.

"Who is she?"

"The flower in the higher sky." He took out a name patch. Sánchez was embroidered on it. "And whose is that?"

"The name belonged to a Saint."

"You haven't mentioned your name, soldier."

"Saint."

"The Saints only passed, but didn't die."

"But this one has."

***

With the permission of the author, this prologue was taken from the book:

Prologue Two

Mia

Thankfully, we arrived in Lombok even earlier than our original schedule. All was the courtesy of Lance. I wouldn't trade him for any other navigator, especially not after he joined our bed. I would keep him.

"Go see, Mandy. We got this, baby girl."

"Your mothership, Sandy."

"Aye." He nodded, giving me a reassuring smile.

"If the governor's princess is the one you're so excited to see, you need to take it outside, Captain." Our Great One pulled his bright sky eyes away from the binoculars. He looked at me with his arms crossed.

Only one of my feet almost stepped outside the primary bridge, so I stopped myself. While moving backwards, I asked him, "Is there anything about her that we should be concerned about? She and I are practically sisters. Not by birth, at least, but close to it. She sounded different on our last phone call. Different bad."

"She isn't my concern. Yours, nonetheless." He turned his body towards Mandy at the port.

"Then I shall see her *outside*, as you wish."

Our Great One continued, "Captain, Older Ceolmund, it's her watchdog that might be concerning for our operation. As far as the princess's safety goes, she's in good hands. But that lone wolf she has can be lethal."

Joe turned his head towards me. I could feel him locking his eyes on me. "Understood, our Great One. I'll help Captain Phinnisee take the measurements."

There were no words coming out of my lips. I didn't know how to respond to that kind of information. I didn't even know what to think.

Mandy had already returned here for almost a year. Even with so many employees in her company, or even with a bodyguard following her everywhere, I could tell that she had been alone. She surely had lost some sleep by the way her panda eyes looked; the dark circles gave some puffiness around her grey eyes. She was restless, escaping from earth into her towering, high paperwork. It was the only escapism she understood. It only became seamless because they were now digital.

"Oh, I've missed you so much, cupcake."

She chuckled. "Please don't tell me you've asked someone to make me some cupcakes."

"Indeed, I have." I took out a cupcake from the box. "No worry, dear. I brought four here, in case you want to get your watchman fat."

She talked with her mouth full of cake. "Owh, Max, this is Mia. Mmhh, it tastes good. I sowwwyy, couldn't help it."

"Saint. Max Saint. Nah, I'm good with the cake. She can have all of them. So where to?"

"Oh, we can't board the ship. They're a bit occupied cleaning up from Australia."

"So I've heard Australia was a bit of a handful. I hope it wasn't out of hands, Captain."

I had no clue what he heard or from whom he heard it. I wondered if this was what the Great One said about him. "Well, each journey has its own challenges. But I'd follow Mandy on this one. We're lucky enough she shoves those cupcakes in her mouth."

"Glad we're on the same boat." He looked at her through the mirror. "Where to, princess?"

"Is there something between them?"

While chewing, she said, "Umh, I trust you, Max."

Immediately, I turned my face towards Mandy. She was always having a hard time trusting people. Either my ears were ringing, so I thought I heard her saying that she trusted him, or there was *definitely* something between them.

She asked me rhetorically, "What?"

"Nothing. Nice to know you've learnt how to trust anyone on planet Earth."

Mandy, indeed, had a birthright to the title, but the way he called her princess was different. It was like he called her *his* princess. And the way her body moved was different around him. She let go of her control so that he could almost Daddy her.

As she said on the phone, he was older than her. I agreed that Max looked like he was 33 years old. But I had met ex-military shadow-workers, so I knew that there was something that he buried underneath those calms before the storm. Either he was actually older or he was on a specific MOS that required him to be unreadable.

Max stopped at a restaurant near the beach. He must had learnt that they served the freshest seafood here. "Is this one okay? People in the office wouldn't know how to handle her sugar rush tomorrow. At least with seafood, she can be as salty as she wishes."

"Of course. She can crack those crabs open. Or cracking open whatever it is she has in her head." I turned to look at her. "Well, you can't be crabby all the time, you see."

"Again, we're on the same boat," Max agreed, implying that we shared the same concerns.

She looked at us in turns before he opened his door. "What is it with you two implying everything in every sentence you speak?"

"Some aspects of seamanship have similar occupational hazards as the armed forces. So we learnt to deliver messages without being caught."

"So, I've heard."

After opening the door for her, he said, "Oh, you got some icing on there. Let me... I got you."

Although I was glad that someone cared for her, nobody paid a bodyguard to care about cake frosting, just like what I saw. The waitress found two tables for us quickly. Mandy and I sat a few tables away from Max. He was sitting towards the front entrance to continue looking out.

Mandy talked a lot about her father's matchmaking plan. So I asked her about how much Max knew about it and if what she said was true about trusting him. At some point in our messy supper, Mandy was struggling to crack the crab open. I locked my eyes on Max's eyes intentionally. Then I looked at my left hand and returned to look at him in the eyes. I could only hope that he would understand.

When Mandy finally cracked open the crab, she continued telling me her story. Somehow, I became more concerned about her now than before meeting her. I went to the loo when I felt full—full from eating and full of thoughts about her.

When I got out of the loo, Max was already there, in the shadow, looking outside, doing his job. "I almost thought you didn't get the message."

"Morse code was one of the basics."

"Did you sign any non-disclosure agreements when you got hired?"

"Yes." He didn't respond further, only anticipating what was needed to be said or asked.

"There's no trust law in this country. Her father was concerned that whoever married her would get his hands on her money. And let's not forget everything her father has once he dies. So he put everything under the holding company. It was done right after her parents' messy divorce."

"I'm listening."

"Also, this country acknowledges that husbands will be the patrons of their wives. Fathers have less power once their daughters are married. So I assume that it was the holding company that hired you on the paper."

"I can neither confirm nor deny your assumption. You've heard me, NDA."

"That's my point. To protect the CEO, *her*, from whoever is potentially harming her. It doesn't matter if it was her future husband *or* her own father."

"Is the princess herself a threat?"

"Your judgement, Saint; if that is even your real name. If it isn't, you better live up to the name."

"Saints patronise and protect."

"Huh, glad to know the 'serve and protect' never left this soldier."

"And you're suggesting what?"

I sighed, delaying my next sentence. "She wasn't built the way we were, Saint. She doesn't even have contingency plans. So she doesn't scatter a little bit of something across the world. If she decides to leave, she'll bring nothing but whatever she wears that day."

***

This prologue was taken from the book:

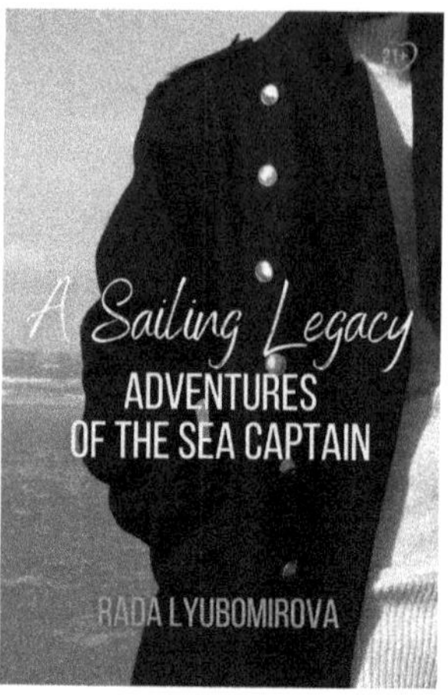

1

Flight Out

Max

Her legs were shaking as I kept her wrists restrained. She tiptoed to support herself. To keep herself in balance. Her body had been stretched up to the ceiling for a while now. I wouldn't touch her until she desperately begged me to.

Her thirst to be used like a disposable prisoner needed to be denied. With her head covered, she could only feel me touching her breasts. "Max, please. I almost can't feel anything."

"You like being captured like this, Ashley? Hmm?"

Her desperate whimper was the one that answered. It was her needy cunt that became the betrayer. Inconsistent; that was what this Boss Babe had become. She had been acting like she didn't need any men in her life while silently begging men to use her in the dark. Her cunt proved the opposite of what she's been portraying to the world.

The sound of my slaps landing on her breasts was to sink into her mind. "Maybe you should quit the campaign of telling the world how useless men are.

Did they know how wet your cunt is right now? Did they know about you begging to be fucked?"

Pushing a finger inside her, I kept my belt closer to her back. I made sure she felt it when I took it off with my other hand. "You want the belt, Ashley?"

"Yes, please. Use it on me, Max." Her wrists were clenching the hanging restraint. "One," she said, starting the counting. She held on to it each time my belt landed on her ass. She kept counting until I completed the eighth. "Eight."

Once her wrists were free, she fell onto my chest. I removed her head cover only to watch her mascara smeared by tears. "Beg me to get you off like a good slut."

She fell farther down to her knees. Her eyes looked at me straight in the eyes. She licked her lips, craving and begging, "Please, Max, I need to come."

While taking out my cock right in front of her, I said, "Let me see how desperate you are to get off."

She bit her lower lip as I wrapped my cock with a condom. She surely felt every ladder my cock had each time I fucked her; I could tell from her moan. If only anyone knew how fucking hurt it was to get these Jacob's ladders, they would think five times before getting them.

Ashley kept begging me to fuck her raw. She said she wanted to feel how they were inside her. She even told me that she was taking the birth control pills religiously. That was what she said, but I wouldn't trust her.

I pulled her up before pushing her against the wall. Hearing her louder moan made me go harder. I rammed her cunt until she came. After that, she no longer had the power to keep herself standing. With her thighs trembling, she fell to her knees once again.

"Stop playing and swallow," I said while pulling her hair. I slapped her across the face before fucking her throat.

She was trying to catch her breath after gagging, "Max—"

Not one more word was allowed to come out of her mouth. I shoved my cock back into her, ramming her face wildly. Taking off the condom once I was close, I sprayed my cum on her face and the floor. "Clean up your mess. Spotless."

Her fingers cleaned up what I spilt on her face, scooping up my release. She licked her fingers clean before getting down to the floor. Just as I told her to, she cleaned everything.

"What a cum slut." I opened her mouth, spitting into her. I helped her get to the chair after I finished with her.

"Max, why can't you stay? Stay with me. For me."

"I can't stay for someone who doesn't need me. Surely you know it'll take both ways to work it out."

"But it's only for social. I'm not like that in real life. You know that, Max. I can take them down if you stay with me."

"Ashley, please tell me you ain't that naive. The internet doesn't easily forget what you post. Once you're on the grid, you're traceable."

"So, what is it then? Are you joining that toxic masculinity movement now? Shaming independent women?"

"Haha. Look, don't get me wrong. My fiancée was a pilot, working around men. She said that we only had 5 percent of women working in the cockpit. Damn, she was a badass. Clearly, I have no problem with women in leadership. But each time she took off her uniform, she was so feminine around me. She let everyone see that." I paused, remembering. "She made me feel like I was coming home after winning a war on duty. I can't get nothing like that from you. You're kinda dismissive of me. To men in general."

She gave me her disgusted, snorting face. "Huh, she sounds like the perfect angel. Kinda ironic that you two are no longer together, right?"

"She's been an angel since the first day we met. She's flying into the higher sky now in Heaven. She must become a much more beautiful angel up there than here on earth. Sometimes, I can almost feel her in the wind."

"*Against the wind. I need to take off and land against the wind,*" Floret said.

Ashley's eyes opened wider in guilty shock. "Max, I'm sor—"

"What I'm saying is, you can't ask me to stay for you and tell the world that you don't need me at the same time. 'Boss babes don't need men,' you said. There you have it; a life without men. None of us would stick around being humiliated publicly like that. That's the price you need to pay for your so-called personal branding."

"Then what do I do to make you stay?"

While rubbing her back, I looked at her. I kept her close to me, as I could feel her regret. "Nothing. Better stick to what you said; that's your integrity in play. You do what you preach, with or without anyone's watching."

"So, just like that? You just leave everything behind? Like, where do you go?"

"Away."

The next thing I knew, I was on a one-way long-haul flight. Returning to equator land. Flying out far away from where I came from, I brought only my Army duffel bag—a reminiscence from the past. Where would I go from there? I had no idea, just one foot in front of the other to keep going.

"Just keep looking forward, Max," Floret said.

She brought my heart with her to the sky. She was flying higher with my soul to Heaven. Only my body remained on earth.

2

Her Governance

Mandy

"It's for your own good, Mandy," my father said. He was in his last year of running the office as governor. With his health declining, he became more persistent about finding me a husband. So far, he had given me two finalists.

"I understand, father. You've raised me well enough for me to know how to run the company. The team is more than capable of sustaining itself on its own. They've been loyal to you as well as to me."

"I trust you to be resilient enough to run the company. Tsk, it's the other half of nurturing that concerns me. Being bought into that feminist nonsense, but she gave up eventually."

"Hmm..."

"What I'm saying is that you're twenty-six already. Should I remind you of being only half English? Here in the East, you should already be married with children by now."

"Father, to make you less worried, I do need a man in my life. And I'd prefer something else that I already had under my bra and knickers."

"Huh, glad to know my daughter is straight. Oh, come on... They don't look that bad. Both of them have the financial stability to take care of you when I'm no longer here. Or maybe you can imagine someone else when you're with either of them."

Through the mirror, I saw Max holding his laughter when he stopped at the red light. "Max, let me see your face."

When leaning forward through the gap in between the front seats, I looked towards Max's face. "Huh, you cute."

Once I returned to my seat, I turned my face towards my father. "I shall be imagining Max when I'm in bed with one of them."

"Your 'not bringing me into this conversation' will be much appreciated," Max said.

"Ooh, I heard Latinos be hot in bed. As if h.o.t. *hot*, father." I leaned forward once again, looking towards my bodyguard. "Have you *ever* cheated on your woman before?"

"Didn't I tell you not to bring me into this? But no, I haven't cheated on anyone. Not my thing."

"Ace, Max. You can marry me now." I leaned back into my seat. I could see my father's remorse when I mentioned disloyalty in the conversation. I was sure he regretted what he did, but it was in the past. Besides, it wasn't my marriage.

"My problem is solved. You see, father, I can trust Max on any given day. But I don't think I'd trust either of those men you're suggesting. Please, Max, take it as a compliment, not an insult."

Max opened my door once we arrived. He walked me from the car to the entrance of the restaurant. "Please make sure he takes his medicines before bed. Shove them down his throat if you have to. You're much stronger than him, that I can tell."

"I'll shove my cock down your throat if you beg me enough, princess." Seeing his smirk, I almost wished that he actually had those words to cross his mind. I could almost see myself on my knees in front of him, begging and obeying him.

"I will. Hey, one more thing. Let him have the benefit of the doubt. I'm only one call away, princess. Ring me if you need me to pick you up."

"All right, Daddy. No, really, I'll be all right." I left him at the entrance. He was still there when I looked over my shoulder. I meant it when I said that I could trust him.

Lyncoln was already with some women near the bar when I walked in. Although I knew them from some initiatives in the past, I wouldn't be so easily trusting them. Especially not Lyncoln, since he always relied on his charms to enchant everyone around him. Definitely not Lyncoln, whom I was marrying, since he said that I should be staying at home to wait for him and raise the children.

Tonight was about my father's initiative in matchmaking. Supper wouldn't hurt, would it? Lyncoln was one of two men that my father chose for me. He had been under my father's wings since he was an intern. My father said that Lyncoln had the capability to make tough decisions.

I was all right until the thought of Max came into my head. Had he not made any tough decisions when he was serving in the Army?

His physique was different from the military men I saw on social media. He wasn't built like a tank, but more for his height. The first time he came to our house, he said that he was 33 years old. He looked like 33 to me.

I was all right until the vision of Max projected itself into my head. When Lyncoln started taking off my dress, I was no longer all right because I could only feel Max's hands stripping me naked.

I was no longer sane when I tasted Max's lips kissing mine and nibbling my hardened nipples. Lyncoln was never inside me; it was my watchman who filled my empty core.

"*Are you awake, Max? Stay with me.*" When releasing for none other than my bodyguard, I was floating in the starry night sky. Tonight, my orgasm was for him. And it wasn't the first time that I gave mine to him.

3

Her Whispering Shadow

Max

"I'm sorry for your loss."

"How could you, Max? Three months? She was on her dying bed, pretending to be strong enough to face death while you were away. You only came here three months after her passing," said her brother.

"I was on deployment."

"Who are you joking here? Your friends were sent home, but not you."

"I was on another assignment. Nevertheless, I truly am sorry for your loss."

"Max, she. was. your fiancée, for fuck's sake! Stop pretending that she wasn't your loss, either."

"Are you awake, Max? Stay with me," Mandy said.

Her voice woke me up. Looking at my watch, it was two in the morning. I fell asleep shirtless on the couch, not in bed, in case she called me.

Vibrating.

Mandy: "Can you please pick me up at 07.30 at Lyncoln's?"

Me: "No sleeping at this hour?"

Mandy: "Why are you not sleeping, Max?"

Me: "You woke me up."

"It was indeed your voice that woke me up, princess."

Me: "Do you want me to pick you up now?"

Mandy: "Max, I'll be all right. I'd say 'good night,' but it's already past midnight. So, sleep tight."

Me: *writing...*

***

Five in the morning. I didn't reply to her text. It wasn't the first time her voice woke me up. Her voice and, at the same time, the hair at the back of my neck suddenly rose.

"Ace, Max. You can marry me now." She shouldn't have said that to me or called me 'Daddy.'

"I'll shove my cock down your throat if you beg me enough, princess." It crossed my mind when I walked her to the lobby. And I shouldn't touch myself while imagining her.

Those gray eyes always looked straight into my eyes when she talked to me. Except when she was drunk, her eyes weren't as sharp. I carried her to bed every time she was wasted. She usually pulled me closer behind her, as if I were her blanket that kept her warm at night. I could have taken her from the back. Maybe I should have. Instead of wasting the cum on my hand like this, I should have emptied my balls inside her.

"Should I break someone's neck or not?"

"Such a telenovela. Thanks for the coffee, by the way." She took a sip of her coffee with a restless face.

"How did you know about telenovelas?"

"We watched telenovelas when we grew up. They were dubbed, of course. Nan said, 'no changing the channel!' Haha." After putting her seatbelt on, she said, "Can you drive me to the office?"

I looked at her through the mirror. "It's Saturday, princess."

"Yeah, I know. I'll take a shower in the office. Did my father take his medicines?"

"Ay, stubborn. Both of you. It's in the genes, I guess. But he took his medicines."

"I should lend you a mirror." She giggled. "Anyway, Mia's ship is harbouring tomorrow evening."

"I'll take you to her."

I brought her something for breakfast, but she almost skipped her lunch that day. Around two in the afternoon, I came to the office to bring her food. It wasn't always easy for her to be a woman in leadership.

It wasn't her company that she built. She was only continuing the legacy, which she kept passing on to her people. She was good at keeping records of how she did something in the company. That started to become her legacy in some way. She built scenarios for the what-ifs and how to solve them.

There was always something that occurred at work, although we both knew that it was her way to escape. Something to bury herself into work. I used to be like her when Floret was gone. Mandy was like me that way, and I was like her.

We were the escapees from our realities. We had the urge to make sure that the ones we left behind would survive the what-ifs once our realities no longer existed.

4

Turnaround

Mandy

On Sunday morning, around nine, Max was driving me to Sawyer's mansion. Except he was turning the car around. "Um, Max. It's *that* way."

"Yeah, I know." He was driving around the complex of mansions. "It didn't sit right with me."

"Of course, it didn't because it's a brunch. You eat right at the right time. It's too late for your breakfast but too early for your lunch. I know, Max. The term 'on time' for the armed forces is late. You're always ahead of time."

"Nah, not that." He pulled over and started massaging his forehead. "I mean, he's filthy rich. And your father wants you well-provided. Well, I get that. I want that for you, too. But there's something off about this Sawyer guy—"

"Too good to be true?" Our eyes met through the mirror. "Tell me not to go, and I won't."

It took him a few moments before he said, "It's not my place, princess."

"You're a man yourself. And I trust you. Tell me which one to marry." By locking our eyes together through reflections, I waited for his answer. A part of me was hoping for him to say his own name.

"As I said, princess, it's not my place."

"Do you believe in the afterlife, reincarnation, rebirth, or whatever you may call it?"

"Yeah, I've been there. Sometimes it's in the same cycle. You know... when they kill someone inside you, and then you're no longer the same person."

Smiling at his reflection, I said, "Maybe in another life you can find me. I'm going to marry you in that life, Max. I meant it when I said that I trust you."

He tilted his head while keeping our eyes locked. He didn't say anything, but I knew he would find me. I knew he would; I knew my watchman that well.

"Now, would you *please* drive me there? I'm starving."

Not a single word came out of his lips. Was I not worth trying in this lifetime? I might be wrong about him.

However, I wasn't wrong about Sawyer. He walked his way towards my father through his connections. To him, I would be another venture conquest with my pussy as a bonus.

He was much older than Lyncoln. Divorced, no children, filthy rich. He deceived others to get what he wanted. He had control over money. So he could control them and tell them what to do, just as he told me to crawl to him. Only in my knickers. On all fours, I was exposing myself to him.

"Your father was right. You *are* beautiful. Once we're married, my colleagues might find you beautiful, too," said Sawyer.

With my head elsewhere, with someone else, I didn't see Sawyer in front of me. I was with someone who, I believed, wouldn't ever share me with anyone.

"He lies his eyes on you one more time, Imma rip off those eyes from his skull." I remembered Max saying it when we were at a party. He thought I wasn't listening because I was drunk. But I was.

I listened to Max when he told me to take a shower before bed. Even if all I wanted was for him to lick me clean, I listened.

I listened to him when he told me to eat every time I almost skipped my meal. Even if all I wanted to swallow was his meat, I listened.

I listened to him when he told me to drink some juice every day. Even if all I wanted to drink was the milk of his release, I listened.

I listened to all that he said when he told me to catch some rest and get enough sleep. Even if all I wanted was to sleep naked in his arms and spend the entire next day hiding under the blanket of his protection, I always listened to my watchman.

5

Leap of Faith

Max

It was half past five on Monday morning. I couldn't even believe Mandy woke up this early in the morning. She was a night owl. Not to mention, it was Monday. If there was anything she loved to do on Monday, that would be wasting the day in the office until late in the night.

She wasn't someone who was scared of the ghouls in the office; more likely, she didn't care. She was more terrified by the men in the dark who were aiming for her. Princess would run to me immediately, fulfilling my personal sense of duty to protect her. I wasn't the knight in shining armor saving her. I was the horrible creature that guarded her in the tower that her father built.

What terrified her the most were cockroaches. She would jump straight onto me, panicking and sobbing; I loved it when she did that. She didn't know that they started to call me a cockroach for being hard to kill. I took it as a compliment; Army jokes were built differently. But, yeah, I'd crawl that damn dirt to survive.

The princess was in her survival mode. That one I could tell from miles away. She skipped breakfast, but not coffee. I was starting to worry about how much caffeine she took daily. But what could I say? She won the stubbornness game; every word I said could be a warzone on any day at any time.

"Ready, princess?"

She sighed. "I give up trying to stop you from calling me that. All right, you win."

"Did she just say that I won?"

I could see her talking inside her head again. But this time she was... different. Concerning. "You should've given up a long time ago. Could've saved you so much energy from arguing with me."

"Hmm..." Nothing else came out of her full, pink lips. She carried her coffee tumbler in her hand and nothing else. She was wearing a white t-shirt, jeans, and sneakers, but no make up. No watch. Not even a hair tie.

"You got your wallet, keys, and phone with you?"

"Why would I need them? I already have you, Max. What could go wrong?"

"Now, that's concerning."

As usual, I opened the car door for her, but she didn't hop in. I closed the door again when she opened the front left door.

When I sat in the driver's seat, she asked, "What?"

I smirked at her. "Nothing. Feel like changing the view today?"

"Can you please drive? Her ship sails early. I want to wave Mia goodbye from the cliff. I only wish she could stay longer. She's been pretty much my older sister. From different parents, but still, well, you were in the armed forces. So, um—"

"Princess, I get your point." I drove out of the gate, heading to the highest ground on the island. I'd never been there myself. "You should have asked your father to buy the cruise ship ticket."

"Oh, let's pretend that we didn't know that my father would be sending you along with me on that thing. What am I planning? A honeymoon cruise on Slava? With you? Aaw... so sweet," she said with an annoying voice.

"Ay, princess. "You gotta pay me hard to keep my mouth shut from telling those princes how annoying you can be."

"Well, that's my savior! My knight in shining armor. He's keeping my secret safe."

She kept herself silent for a while, and then she fell asleep on the half-way drive. She didn't behave like this. It made me curious about the conversation she had with Mia last night.

Her friend Mia had been the captain of Slava for about four years now. The first time I knew about the ship was about five years ago. Not everything that I saw or heard was reported, especially if it came from a hunch. I'd always been suspicious about that ship; she was almost too good to be true. Not every ship could sustain a long sail with so much power but so little fuel. But she could. An ocean liner that could pass through *any* conflicting territories and get away untouched? Any conflicting side just gave her a way. Just like that?

It would be nice if I could take a look at what's inside her. Well, I was no longer in the Army, so I no longer had to report anything to anyone. Not because I cared, but just for the what-if. What if my hunch was right over the years?

After I parked the car, I took a few minutes to let her sleep a bit more. There was something about her today that tickled my nerves. I'd never seen her loosen like this. I'd seen her without any make up, but not like this morning.

The hair at the back of my neck rose once again. There was something about what she said earlier, *"Why would I need them? I already have you, Max. What could go wrong?"*

She wasn't like that. Not on *that* level of surrendering. She was fierce, especially when defending her friends or anyone who needed defending. She was also brave for keeping her ground when facing the princes. She kept herself grounded, even if her time was ticking to choose one of them. The limited choice of men that her father made her choose.

Just as she asked yesterday, I agreed in silence. I would have wife her up in another life, granting her wish. At this moment, she wasn't being herself. I didn't want to lose her under my watch.

"I don't want to lose you, princess."

"Princess, we're here," I said, waking her up from her nap. I wished I could run my fingers through her hair when I woke her up.

She took a sip of her coffee in silence. "What time is it? Did I drool?"

I gave her the wet tissue from the compartment box. "A quarter past six. Here, for your drool." She wasn't drooling, but I continued teasing her.

"What would I do without you, Max?" That was her second one of the day.

"Probably dead in under a minute. Other than that, I think you'd be just fine." I didn't know if I could contain myself if there was a third one coming.

"Yeah, just fine. But everyone's expecting much more than *just fine* from me, in case you haven't noticed." She put down her tumbler before saying, "Can I have a hug, please?"

"*Oh, fuck yes! I'd fuck you properly in the back seat with that 'good girl please' you just said.*" The thought I had for this beautiful princess was *that* crazy. She was indeed beautiful.

"I don't think we should, princess. Are you sure you're alright?"

"Pfft... It's not like we've never hugged before. In the crowd, party, remember?"

"I was guarding you from those drunk assholes—"

Just like that, she dropped her head on my chest, hugging me tightly. Her father would get me in so much trouble if he knew that I was hugging her back.

"I got you, princess. Everything's gonna be alright. I promise." Instead of letting her go, I combed her hair with my fingers.

"You can be quite annoying sometimes. But other than that, you're just fine."

We walked to the higher ground, towards the cliff. It was kind of nice to have this view in the morning. We just sat there in silence. I didn't know what was going on inside her head.

"You're overthinking it again, princess."

"What should I do then? To take a leap of faith just like that?" That stare she gave me was piercing. She had been doing it to me lately. Straight in the eyes, down to my soul, she got my cock to salute its commander in chief.

"You know how stubborn you are. I can't tell you what to do or what not to do."

She sighed her burdens out, but she still tried to give me a smile. "Max, I forgot my coffee in the car. Can you please get it for me? Please."

That 'please,' once again. I didn't think she realized what she'd done to my cock. "I'll get it for you."

I was locking the car door when I heard the horn of Slava broadcasting a distress signal. She was cruising from my left towards the cliff where Mandy stood. I squinted my eyes, seeing the captain on the glass-covered bridge.

Through her binoculars, she was looking towards Mandy. Then she turned towards me. It was weird that the captain wasn't only turning her face but also turning her entire body towards me. Putting down her binoculars, she placed her hand on her heart.

I squinted my eyes even more at the captain and even took a few steps forward. I didn't know what it meant. Then I heard the horn blow again.

A much stronger message was blown this time. Immediately, I turned my face towards Mandy.

Seeing her running and finally jumping off the cliff, I dropped her coffee in an instant. I was running as fast as I could to the cliff where she was standing.

"Please, please, please, I can't lose you, too, Mandy. Please."

I kept running until I finally took my leap. For her.

6

Her Death; Our Rebirth

Max

Ditching in the water, I started to search for her. She was nowhere, as far as I could see. These fucking seaworms didn't get to help me find her easily. Red, green, and every color in between. They were everywhere, swarming from and towards every direction.

Nearly out of breath, I then went to the surface for some air. Every second felt like a thousand years. "Mandy... Princess?"

I took the deepest breath that I could before diving into the water again. Swimming farther, I kept searching for her. There, I saw her.

"Who the fuck is that man?" He was huge, even bigger than me. He was cupping her face and kissing her lips. He didn't give her air but only kissed her while her face was still.

"Fuck! She's far down."

I went to the surface one more time to take another deep breath before swimming as fast as I could towards her. She was right there in stillness. The man was no longer there.

Once I reached her, I pinched her nose and blew some air into her mouth. This wasn't what I imagined our first kiss would be. I wrapped my arm around her, holding her back. I pumped her chest with my other hand. I didn't even know if it was working.

Blowing another breath of air into her, I tried one more time. *"Please come back to me, princess."*

Here she was, coughing up the air I blew. She came back from her stillness. Cupping her face, I blew another breath into her. While I was rubbing my thumbs on her cheeks, she held my wrists gently.

With my hands still cupping her face, I blew my last breath into her. That smile was worth it; let her have my end. All I needed to see at the end of my time was her beautiful face.

Letting her go, I let the depths of the sea have me. I felt the seaworms swarming on my skin when my eyes started to close. Let them have me. And let my princess live.

A punch in the chest—that was what I felt next. Someone shoved something into my mouth. The diver gave me a sign to inhale the oxygen.

There were many of them; I didn't know how many exactly. All of them were wearing blue drysuits. No one—I meant no one—should ever wear the color blue for swimming or diving. The fact that they were wearing blue only meant that they were in stealth mode. They intentionally did not want to be seen.

I hadn't learned Bisindo, but I spell-signed her name and asked where she was with ASL.

"Holy shit! The diver replied with ASL. Who the fuck are they?" He signed back, "To the net."

It wasn't the season for sea worm fishing; that would be on the twentieth day of the tenth month in their traditional calendar. *"Then, what net?"*

Still, I swam following them.

"Oh, fuck!" There were giant nets to fish these divers out. We were the catch. Those seaworms were just an added bonus, I guessed.

After we boarded the ship, the first thing I read was "SLAVA. DECK 1." They pulled me in to follow the stream of the crowd. Whatever this was, it was clearly organized by pros.

We entered a hall where they slipped off their drysuits. Underneath, they were wearing suits, as if they were professional bodyguards. Much more polished than mine, the high society type of suit from the Regency movie.

"Max!" She was running towards me. "I thought I had lost you," she said with a concerned face.

"I thought I had lost you. The fuck were you thinking, princess? You should be grateful these people were around."

"Ah, there they are, the lovebirds fighting," said the huge man, entering the room.

"Why didn't you help her down there? You were just there, trying to kiss her or something. She could have died."

"Because that's my Duty, after all." His sky like eyes started to flare.

Middle East at one time. Eastern Europe at one other time. I nodded to the Angel of Death.

"Huh, he remembers me now. What happened to that soldier after... Lani, was she?"

"Dead. He's no more."

"Is that so? I can't recall taking you. Well, in case you forgot, this one was unnaturally giving her life up. We brought her up here only because you were so desperately trying to bring her back."

"We appreciate your help."

"I see you've changed your uniform for a suit. You can stay. Unfortunately, we need to think about what to do with her. Besides, she couldn't care less about keeping her life."

I pulled Mandy closer behind me, then pulled my gun out towards the Angel of Death himself.

"Um, Max," said Mandy while squeezing my arm.

Turning my face towards her, I could see those people pointing their guns at her head.

"Your gun is wet, soldier. Theirs aren't." He slammed my gun and pulled my forearm closer to him. "Be grateful for my generosity. As I said before, you can stay. You've got the skills for shadow-working, but she doesn't. And she's seen too much already."

"She—she's my wife."

Tilting his head, he said, "Her face is in shock. Either that's news even for her *or* you're such a horrible husband that made her jump off of that cliff only to escape you."

"Her father wouldn't approve of us. He hired me as her bodyguard, but I never touched her."

He was smirking at Mandy behind me. "Is that so, young lady?"

"My father said that I could choose between two men. Max wasn't one of them. Um, I couldn't make the choice."

He sighed at her words. "Well, we need to work on your decision making skills. So far, you've made poor decisions."

He took off the amulet from his neck. Hanging the necklace with one hand, he held the amulet inside the fist of his other hand. "Since her dear father isn't here, you can brand her as your wife."

One woman was pushing Mandy closer to me after locking her arms on her back. Another woman pulled her t-shirt up to her ribs.

"Your right palm. Brand her on the left rib with this. That is, *if* you choose to make her your wife."

Mandy was panting with a confused face. "Max?" Her eyes opened wider when she saw me put my right palm up. Her chest was moving up and down faster when I received the burning, hot amulet.

"MAX...!" She screamed my name out of her lungs when my palm pushed the amulet against her rib. It was so hurtful to see her hurt like this. Way more hurtful than the amulet did hurt me.

She was shaking when I pulled it from her rib. Her feet were trembling before I caught her from falling. My knuckles rubbed her cheek, wiping her tears away. "My wife now, princess."

"Hhh... Max—" She passed out. My name; she screamed my name and nothing else.

"Congratulations on your marriage."

He looked at those women who had held her before. "Would you mind taking her to the medical center? Also, check yourselves with the doctor while you're there, will you?"

"We will, our Great One."

"All of you, after you see the doctors, please go to Deck 6 as soon as you can. I can't have those cupcakes all by myself, can I?" He said it to them with compassion, as if he truly cared about his people.

One of them gasped. "Milady baked cupcakes? Yup, heading Deck 6." He walked out of the hall immediately.

"Hey, I said *after*. Oh my word, these younglings. What would I do with the sugar rush after?"

"Surely we can give the groom his warm welcome," said another one of them.

"Ah, marvellous. A*fter* he is cleared by the doctor, of course." He left me with his people.

7

Switching Sides

Max

They walked me into the medical center. They kept me close, as if I would run out of here without my wife. My princess just became my wife. I couldn't tell if she'd be upset or pleased when I addressed her as my wife later.

I saw her lying on one of the beds. I turned to one of them, asking, "Am I allowed to ask the doctor about her?"

He nodded his approval. "Let the doctor check you while you're there."

I walked towards her bed. "How is my wife, doctor?"

"Firstly, congratulations on your marriage. Secondly, we ran her blood test but needed to wait for the result. We treated the burning wound. This waterproof dressing is so she can take a shower later."

"And how should I care for her after she wakes up?"

"In a few days, we'll open this. Then you can apply the ointment to it. I need to read her test result before making any decision."

"Understood. Thank you for your help."

"Have a seat. Let me check on you."

"I'm alright, doctor."

"It's standard procedure here. You need to get tested as well. I'll ask them to retrieve your medical record." He started by treating my right palm.

"I'm a blank canvas. They scratched my records when I was in the Army."

He chuckled at me. "Clearly, you're new. You have no clue about the institution, don't you? These shadow-workers, they're *that good* at doing their job. So, they *will* retrieve your records." He took my blood and saliva for testing in tubes.

"But she'll be alright, won't she?"

"She'll need some rest for now."

I kept holding her hand while the doctor was doing his work. I was kissing the back of her hand when a shadow-worker came near us.

"Oh, fuck me! Please don't tell me First Sergeant Saint's switching sides." He paused to stare at my sleeping wife. "Really? For a woman? I can't blame you, though. She's cute."

"Wife. Do I know you somewhere?"

"Duly noted. She's off the market. Ooo... we better give this one the warmest welcome. Your fireworks almost got me. Almost, but didn't. Don't flatter yourself too high. Falling hurts."

The doctor smirked at me. "Someone will watch and care for her while you're in training. You should be worried about yourself. The codes that the institution holds are different than in your previous branch."

"I'd appreciate your care for her, doctor. How's the code different?"

"Let's say more grayish, but the suits are more polished. The suits are the uniforms for the shadow-workers. You'll learn along the way. One last thing before I send you back to them. We need you to get checked daily after your training before going to your quarter."

"Everything's gonna be alright, princess. I'll go home to you after training. Have a rest so you can get better soon," I whispered in her ear. I kissed her hand one last time before turning myself to the shadow-workers.

"This way, First Shirt. Oops, I forgot, Shirt's changing to wearing a suit. No ranks applied here."

I didn't give him any response. Instead, I walked to wherever they led me. All these times, my suspicions were right about Slava.

"What's the institution they're at? What are those so-called shadow-workers doing besides being mercenaries? Fuck, this ship must cost billions of dollars to build. What did the Angel of Death have to do with it? Did he build it? Who is this 'Milady'?"

8

A New Life

Mandy

I woke up in a hospital bed with other patients nearby. "Um, Max?"

"It's all right, Mrs. Saint. You're in the medical centre," said a nurse.

It felt surreal to hear someone address me as his missus. I looked around and asked, "What time is it?"

"Just past noon. Your husband is in training with other shadow-workers."

"Training?"

"It's sort of a basic indoctrination for newcomers. Some of them are also in retraining, so there's a chance that he'll be joining one of those."

"What are you giving me?"

"Mineral infusion for now. The doctor will come to visit once your test results come back. Then he will make further decisions."

"Test for what?"

"For everything. It's our standard for shadow-workers and their kin. We take care of each other's families as well. You should get some rest so you can recover soon." She left me and returned to her station.

My husband. Max married me this morning. I should be fuming at him for branding me. Somehow, I felt relieved. I was glad that it was him and not anyone else; Max always had my back.

I didn't know what they gave me, but I was feeling oddly sleepy. My eyes got heavier and heavier with every second passing.

***

Someone was strapping my arms; I felt it. There were a doctor and a nurse visiting my bed. "Am I low?"

"Yes, you have low blood pressure. Do you usually have it low?"

"Mostly, yes. I sometimes skip meals when working. Max kept checking to see if I had eaten yet. Um, how are my test results?"

"Nothing to worry about, but you need to have your meals on time and be well-rested for recovery. Do you exercise regularly?"

"I do it a few days a week, but I keep changing my routines from time to time. I got bored easily sometimes."

"Keep exercising, then. Each person has their own preference. Are you on any birth control?"

"I've been on pills until yesterday. I didn't bring anything when I left. Only Max."

"I can send you to OBGYN if you need a replacement. She'll be in her office in the morning."

"It's better if I talk to my husband first about this. Did his test results come out yet?"

"His tests are different than yours. He's done a preliminary check, the same as yours. He needs to be checked again this evening. We scheduled him for a complete health exam the day after tomorrow."

"I'll remind him about that."

"You also need to come here on the same day. So we can check your wound. The nutritionist and I made a list for your diet. Let us know if you have any food allergies."

"Thank you, doctor."

"You can go after having your supper. A crew will come in about an hour to lead you to your quarter. You can ask the crew about the ship. Oh, one moment, please."

He left me to go to the next room and came back not long after. "This should fit his size in the meantime, before you two decide anything."

I nodded and gave the doctor a decent smile, since I didn't know how to react to it. "Thank you again."

Even though I knew that I had to, my stomach didn't feel like eating a heavy meal. Max was in training, they said. Honestly, I had no clue what that meant.

A hospitality crew came in later on. She carried one medium duffel bag and one large one. Emilia looked much younger than me. She helped me put a robe on top of the patient scrub I was wearing.

"Here is your quarter at Starboard. We're on Deck 3 Aft, just in case you're lost. Let me put the bags down first."

"They are for us?"

"This one is yours, and the other one is your husband's. I was told that he's in training. So I prepared his clothes more than yours."

"I truly appreciate your assistance, Emilia."

"No, please, don't mention it. It's the standard. You have four days of clothing, but he has six. A set of suits will be delivered after he passes his health exam." She handed me the key to our quarter.

We had a bathroom with a shower, a small dining table for two, a small refrigerator, a wardrobe, and a bed for two. I never imagined sleeping together with Max in the same bed.

"Let me show you the shared kitchen. It's not far from here."

"Please. After you." I locked the door before we went. Following her through the ship aisle like this felt like walking on a tightrope.

"So the restaurant and kitchen are open 24/7. A chef and restaurant crew are always around here to help, but you can cook by yourself anytime. You need to place the dirty ones inside the dishwashing machine. Laundrettes are also open 24/7 on Decks 0, 2, and 4 for those who live in quarters."

She showed me the way to the kitchen tool storage and coolers. The pantry and coolers were stocked as if this place served as a shop for us to choose from.

"Um, Emilia... I didn't bring anything with me when I left. I don't think my husband was prepared, either."

She gave me an adorable, warm smile and said, "Many of us here fled our origins as runners and escapees. They're free for us to eat. The Great One and his wife take care of all of us here. We call her 'Milady,' and she cooks a lot when she's on board."

She led me to return to the quarter. "Here is my quarter number. You can ask me in the morning if you have any questions."

The sea water had gotten my skin and hair sticky. Everything was prepared inside the bathroom, from body wash to shampoo to conditioners to dental needs. I took a shower, and it felt much better once I finished showering.

They must have measured me when I was passing out. Everything inside the duffel bag was my exact size. Still in my towel, I arranged my clothes in the wardrobe.

"Do I put my clothes on or do I not for Max?"

9

The Beginning of Us

Mandy

I decided to be fully clothed. Max could take them off of me if he wanted to. Looking into his duffel bag, I realised that I knew nothing about him. Nothing about his shirt size, trousers, or footwear; I didn't even know his weight.

He must be around 181-183 cm, because I was around his chest. It was quite funny to figure him out from the things they gave us. Piece by piece, I arranged his clothes in the wardrobe.

Staring at a pack of condoms the doctor gave me earlier, I wasn't sure what he'd think about them. Or about me. I wasn't even sure what this marriage would make him feel like.

"Is he a razor or cut through blade type?" There was a complete set of men's grooming tools and supplies in the bag. The bathroom had a first aid cabinet with a mirror on it, so I arranged both of them inside.

I was placing the hair clippers on the top shelf of the wardrobe when he came in. He caught me right before I completely fell off the chair. "Can you not fall from anywhere again? What were you doing on a chair this late? You should be asleep already."

"Thanks for these little legs, I needed a chair to put the hair clippers they gave you. And thanks to you branding me, I couldn't reach too far up. Here, put them yourself, top shelf," I said while pushing the box to his chest. Pulling the chair, I put it in its spot. "You can't blame me for everything all the time, you see. You—"

In a rapid move, he placed his hand on my neck. Not as tight as choking me to death, but enough to make me listen to him when he said, "I stole you from the Angel of Death. Every breath of air you take into those lungs belongs to me, princess. Before you breathe out a single word from this mouth, remember that this mouth belongs to me. It's for me to kiss, to fuck, or to fill it with my cum."

Those words hit my core in an instant. I didn't know how he did it. My pulsing pussy told me to surrender myself to him. "Mmh... Max." "That's right. You can always moan my name. Screaming my name would be better. Tell me, what are you?"

"Yours, Max. I'm yours," I moaned my answer.

"Keep that in mind, princess." He slowly released my neck from his grip. If that was the hand necklace those women were into, Max just made me realise that I was one of those women. After taking off his shirt, he continued to take off his trousers. There were bruises all over his body.

"Um... Max? Hav—have you eaten anything?"

"I'll be all right." Before stepping into the bathroom, he was completely naked before me. Even from behind, he made me want to join him inside. Maybe I should have joined him.

Once he was in the shower, I prepared a set of underpants, a t-shirt, and tracksuits on the bed for him. I went out to the kitchen as fast as I could to get something for him to eat.

They had rice in the warmer. I took some rice and chicken stew and put them in the container. Hot tea for his drink and some ice packs for his bruises.

He was still shirtless when I entered our quarter. "Thanks for preparing the clothes."

"Chicken stew and rice for tea. They got ice packs, too." I set up his food and cutlery on the table.

He held my hand, saying, "You didn't have to."

"I insist. There's no point in arguing this late. Chop, chop, you'll have more training tomorrow."

He used the ice pack with his left hand while eating with his right. "What did the doctor say about you?"

"I need to get checked again the day after tomorrow. The same day as your health exam." I took the ice pack from him and placed it in the same spot. This way, he could eat easier. He might say that he was all right, but he needed to eat right for his training. "And you? Did you get the evening check?"

"I'll survive. No need to worry about me. I'll take care of everything with the training and with the job after."

"Hmm..." I sighed heavily and left him at the table. Taking his white shirt, trousers, and a hanger with me, I left our quarter to go to the laundrette. It was fine with me if he didn't want to talk.

"Excuse me, miss. Where—"

"Laundrette? Port Aft."

I was frowning on my forehead for not knowing what it meant. "Um..."

"Let me show you where it is. Oh, before we go. This side is the Starboard of the ship; this one is the Port. That part is Forward, but this part is Aft. You need to think of it as the ship herself, not from your perspective."

"Starboard, Port, Forward, and Aft. Got it. I'm sorry, I'm new here."

"Everyone starts somewhere in life."

We entered the laundrette with so many washers and dryers. She showed me where the supplies were and how to use the machines. I thanked her before she left me. I ironed Max's clothes for tomorrow while having my mind travel elsewhere.

***

Max

"The newlyweds are fighting already?"

I didn't respond to him. That's clearly none of his business. I continued placing used flatware into the dishwasher. "Shouldn't you live on the upper deck?"

"I switched my suite with mum's, on Deck 5. Her friends are mostly on Deck 3, and she'll be offboarding tomorrow. So she cooked a *lot* of chicken stew. She'd be murdering me with her flip flop if I didn't come here."

"Oh, that was your mom's cooking? It was delicious, by the way. Please send our thanks to her." I paused, frowning. "Wait, you got thrown flip flops, too? I thought it was a Latina mami thing."

He shook his head. "Asian Mum thing as well. Though Amma isn't really my mum. I'm an orphan, actually. One Chinese sailor found me with a note saying, 'Lance.' That was it, nothing else. I called him Appa Zhou, and he gave me his name. Amma used to work on the same ship with him. They sort of raised me. And you? Are your parents still alive?"

"They were gone when I was a teenager. I found a bookworm in the library I used to work at. Her father gave me a job mowing his farm. Then I got into the Army and proposed to her at one time. Her mother passed away from breast cancer, but she did from ovarian."

"Bruv, I'm sorry."

"Nah, it was a long time ago. I buried myself in duties after that. When I quit the Army, I kinda didn't know what to do. So I left and got a bodyguard job from the governor, watching his daughter. Now she's my wife."

"She's Asian, isn't she?"

"Half-English from her mother. Why?"

"Well, her Asian gene might be stronger than her European one. You'd better not change employers after this. Otherwise, the missus will start learning to use flip flop. 'Murdered by flip flops' wouldn't be glorious, would it?"

"Haha, no, it wouldn't."

"However, I'm glad to see we survived."

"From life or flip flops?" It was nice to have something to laugh at about life. Then I returned to our quarter after that conversation with the second mate.

Mandy returned with my clothes ironed. Here she was, with her thoughts floating in her own conversations. It had been so long since the last time I was in a relationship. I was supposed to be married to Lani. That, too, was a long time ago.

"Are you done there? I need to use the loo."

"Have a go."

Once she was in the bathroom, I opened the cupboard. My shirt, pants, and boxer briefs are hung together on one hanger for tomorrow. Closing the cupboard, I saw it at a glance, and then I paused.

"Did they give her a pack of condoms? Or was she asking for them?"

It was the flushing sound that brought me back. There were so many thoughts on how I'd take her senseless in bed. Moving away from the cupboard, I locked the quarter door.

"Max, don't lock the door yet. I need to put away the food container and cutlery."

"Already done. I met the second mate there. It was his mom who cooked the stew. Well, adopted mom. You should take a rest." I took off my t-shirt and laid myself in bed. I watched her take off her bra without taking off her t-shirt. She should have taken off all of them if it was up to me.

She climbed up the bed, facing the wall on my right. "I'll look for Mia tomorrow. To ask if there's any vacancy on the ship. Good night, Max."

"Good night, princess." I guessed no taking her tonight. But that was all right, because she needed to rest after what the doctor told me. She made it a habit to skip meals. That needed to change, and she needed to listen to me now.

"Um, Max, who is Lani? But it's alright if you don't want to talk about her. You're no longer working for my father."

"We were engaged at one time. Leilani, but people called her Lani. I called her Floret because Lei means flower, and Lani means sky. Yeah, I guess she became a flower blossoming in Heaven."

"Max, I'm s—" she said while rolling her body towards me.

I stopped her from talking or rolling towards me. "No, don't roll this way. Better you sleep that way so your wound stays upright."

"Um, okay." She paused before continuing, "Have you met anyone, you know, after her?"

Reaching around, I lifted her neck and slid my right arm underneath her. "She was the last woman I made love to. One was close to it, but just crossed paths. But yes, fucked some women after she's gone, if that's what you're asking."

My left hand slid under her t-shirt, feeling her wound dressing. My hand kept moving to her stomach to wrap her tightly. Pulling her closer to me like this was only a way to remind her that she was mine.

"Oh, Max, where do we go from here?" The sound of her moan always made my cock twitch.

"We put one foot in front of the other, one step at a time. I will take care of you from now on, princess. Now, tell me what the doctor said. You can't keep things from me anymore."

"They gave me a list to add to my diet. I had low blood pressure, as usual. I easily fainted, as usual. But you know that already."

I kept rubbing her belly to calm her down. One day, I'd fill it with my baby. "You better listen to what they said. They got the licence to practice. And what else did they say?"

"Our next doctor's appointment is the day after tomorrow. Um, Max... thank you."

"For what?"

"For trying. I know I'm not easy to handle sometimes."

I chuckled at her words. "Ay, *princesa*. I haven't even started manhandling you yet. Let alone doing it properly."

10

Vacancy

Mandy

Mia must be having a busy day ahead as a captain, so I woke up as early as I could. Deck 13 was high and far from our quarter. Since Max hadn't had any ID or nameplate, nor had I gotten a job, I was being stopped many times on my way to see Mia. I was told to see her in the captain's suite instead of going to the primary bridge.

A male crew opened the door for me. "Oh, hey! It's the newlyweds. I met your husband last night. Come in, please. Mia's still getting dressed. I'm Lance, by the way." He must be the second mate Max was talking about.

"You can call me Mandy. Please send our gratitude to your mum for her cooking."

"She's offboarding this morning, so I need to go. But I'll tell Amma." He was wearing his shoes and getting ready. "However, congratulations on your wedding. You're in good hands now."

"Thank you."

"Take it easy on him. We, as orphans, sometimes don't know how to act in a relationship. We're used to standing on our own. Different from person to person, of course."

"But you know how to act in bed. And in other places, too," said Mia. They kissed passionately as spouses before he went. That made me envious of them. "Have you gotten any breakfast?"

"No, I haven't. I went here as early as possible. I don't want to bother you at work. You're my friend, but right here you're the captain."

"Oh, please. Let's get breakkie." We left her suite together. "You slept okay?"

"Need adjustment of the marriage life. It's Max we're talking about. He keeps things to himself so much."

She looked around before whispering, "Did you two fuck yet?"

"Honestly, that's what you want to know? Unbelievable. Why did you ask?"

"Only one day you are here, and they're already talking." We stepped aside before entering the restaurant on Deck 11, where the guests ate. "Do you have any clue who he was? You know, before watching you."

Shaking my head, I said, "No, Mia. I know him only as Max Saint. It was only yesterday that I heard the name Lani. Let alone finding out that he's an orphan from your Lance minutes ago."

"You what?" We paused, waiting for some guests to pass. As the captain, Mia greeted them with a warm smile.

"Mia, what did you hear? Really, I'm not even sure if he meant it with this marriage. I'm clueless about who he was or who he is. Am I in trouble of some kind?"

We took our plates of breakfast in silence. It was a quite busy morning because Slava was docking in a touristy place. Guests would both offboard and board at the same time. We found a secluded table outside, away from other guests.

"Mandy, you're my friend. We've known each other long enough for me to see you as my baby sister. Try to look at this from our perspective, yeah? On one hand, spouses could be seen as potential acquaintances. On the other hand, he could be using you to infiltrate our ship. That's why I asked you if you two had sex last night. It was the first night of your marriage."

"We slept in the same bed, but we haven't."

"Well, that's my point. Do you know what I mean?" She sighed. "I don't want him to hurt you."

I nodded to her and kept eating my breakfast. Although there was a storm starting to build in my stomach, I tried to keep myself together. "Then what do you think I should do?"

"For now, watch him closely and listen to him with your ears wide open. Try to pay attention to how he moves or what he says. Details about him."

"I will. And what else did you hear from others?"

"They sort of know him, I think. Either they've worked together when he was in the Army or he used to hunt those shadow-workers down. That needs further leads. Other than that, his dick piercings have made headlines so far."

Gasping while not knowing if I should be concerned or excited, I asked, "Plural? How would they know?"

"Well, basic indoctrinations could mean a broad spectrum, depending on the entry level of the person. I assumed that your beloved pierced husband got mid-up skills or experience that made them strip him naked for, let's say, questioning."

"So that's where the bruises came from. Mia, honestly, what are they doing for their work?"

"We call them projects. They do what is necessary for the projects. Sometimes, and most of the time, those projects come from whichever government needs to keep their hands clean."

"Like mercenaries?"

"Some other times, we help each other who needs some favour. But the Great One and his wife have very strict rules of ethics about what project to take or not to take."

"Um... I'm not sure how to ask it but—"

"You need a job? To keep you of sound mind?"

Nodding. "But, you know, I didn't bring anything with me. So I don't have any documents or things as proof."

"You're as good as dead to the outside world. See this as a rebirth for you. If Max passes his training, you two could be given new identities. But in the meantime, you can write a CV and send it to the Capital and Investing Department."

"Capital and Investing?"

"Yes, we call them CID. The institution sees HR as a human capital department. Every training or upgrade is an investment in human resources. No lies on the CV. They are *that* good at finding out."

"Is there any office or computer that I can use to write my CV?"

"I'll show you the library after we finish eating."

"I appreciate that, Mia. I really do."

"Anyway, I haven't congratulated you on getting married. But I insist on details once you two fuck. Well, after."

"Not a chance. Sue me if you dare."

"Oh, come on, Mandy."

***

Reading the CV I wrote, I kept adding and deleting items for over two hours now. I was used to writing different resumes for different companies or positions. I wasn't quite sure what kind of entity this institution was.

I had no problem adding my time working as a barista in different coffee shops. London was expensive at that time. Besides, I needed to help mum while the divorce from my father hadn't been finalised. I tried to remember everything I had from Uni and the volunteering that I did for others. I was having a hard time building a chronological CV without having references to look up to.

"Ah, I forget about volunteering in teaching and research. Should I add all the research I help with?"

"You look rather stressed out over there. You okay?"

Turning my head towards a man sitting at the opposite table, I said, "I'm writing my CV. Do you know where I can get something to save this file? That'll be extra work if I lose it. I can barely remember anything to write at the moment."

He smirked before leaving the table for the librarian's desk. He came back with a new pack of drives. "You can use this. I'll tell the shop crew later." He opened the wrapping for me.

"I appreciate this."

"May I see it? After you save it, of course."

"Yeah, sure." I watched him read it in silence. I wasn't sure if it would land me a chance.

"*Зовите меня Коля.*" ("Call me Kolya.")

"*Очень Приятно. Меня зовут Мэнди.*" ("Nice to meet you. My name is Mandy.")

"*Вы новенькая здесь? С кем?*" ("You new here? With who?")

"*С мужем. Мы пришли вчера.*" ("With my husband. We boarded yesterday.")

He frowned before saying, "*С днём свадьбы!*" ("Happy wedding day!") He said it in the most flat, sarcastic way.

I wondered how everyone on this ship possibly knew that Max and I got married, although it was useless to hope for answers. Nodding and smiling should be enough to fulfil all the necessities of this conversation.

"*Имеет высшее экономическое образование. Выучила русский, немецкий и итальянский языки в университете.*" ("Degrees in Economics. You learnt Russian, German, and Italian in the University.")

"Мне хочется учить испанский." ("I'd like to learn Spanish.")

"Вам учиться с мужем. Он преподавал испанский язык солдатам в Восточной Европе. Вы учите испанский умом русскоязычного." ("You should learn with your husband. He taught Spanish to soldiers when he was in Eastern Europe. You learn Spanish as a Russian speaker.")

"Чего?" ("Excuse me?")

"Ааа... она не знала, что её муж говорит по-русски." ("Huh, she just found out her husband speaks Russian.")

("Um, anyway, what do you think about my CV? Is it all right to get a job here?")

("Write what you can. You can send it to the CID in Deck 7. They will cross-check what you wrote with the data they can find.")

("I appreciate your help.")

("One more thing. You need to write the quarter where you live. They will send the news there.")

I printed my CV and cover letter after the conversation ended. The crew that received my application was nice. She asked me if there was any other information I needed to add to the application.

11

Making a Home

Mandy

On my way back to the quarter, I found cleaning products for our place. I heard him coming while I was arranging vanities in the bathroom. "I met this man, Kolya, in the library. He said that he knew you from work back then."

"Yeah? He flirts with my wife, or what?"

"He helped me write and print my CV. What is it with you?"

"Doing husband stuff."

I sighed and said, "I'm trying, you see. I can't be here doing nothing while waiting for you. Besides, you'd be living your dreamy, young, free, and single life by now if it weren't for me."

"Nah, I've done that boring kinda life."

I closed the first aid cabinet and wiped the mirror clean. "Then I gave my application to CID. They said that they'd read along and tell me which department needed a crew. There, it's clean now. I'll get supper for us while you shower." I washed my hands before getting out of the bathroom.

"I thought you ate already. You don't need to wait for me. Eat whenev—"

"Oh, my days! Max, what happened? Are you all right?" His face was bruised and swollen. The cut on his lips, however, teased me to lick the blood clean from him. "What do you need? What do I do?"

"You should see the other guy, princess. But yeah, you can keep being a cute wife with that worried face." He chuckled as if it were funny to see me concerned about him. He held the side of my neck while rubbing his thumb on my cheek. "Go get us some dinner. You need to eat, too."

I went to the kitchen and got three food containers and a shopper bag. It was the better way to carry them all at once. Each one of the containers was for a different type of food. I got some rice, some broccoli cap chay, and two pieces of chicken. Also, I brought two plates and cutlery for us to eat. Of course, not to forget the ice packs for Max.

He was still in the bathroom when I entered the quarter. He needed to eat right for his training, so I got him the biggest piece of chicken I could get.

"From now on, no waiting for me to eat, no skipping meals," he said when getting out of the bathroom, only in his towel.

Pretending to set up the cutlery, I tried to look away when he was taking away his towel and putting his clothes on. "You don't need an hour of shower like me, Max. Waiting a few minutes wouldn't be that bad."

"My household, my rule. You eat whenever you need to. Or want to, whichever comes first."

"What? No. I'll be huge like hippo if I listen to you."

"What do you mean? I like my meat chewy. Anyway, I appreciate you cleaning our place." He called it 'our place,' just like we were actually a married couple. So much of it made me want to believe that it was real. I wondered if he believed it, too.

After we finished our meal together, I helped him use the ice packs on his bruises and swells. I brushed my teeth and washed my face after. I felt hurt seeing him come back like this from training.

He insisted on putting the used containers, plates, and cutlery into the dishwashing machine. He cleaned himself before going to bed with me. For the rest of the night, he slept, hugging me tightly in his arms. Not like the previous night, this time he hugged me tightly as if he were holding his life onto me.

I woke up in the middle of the night, only to be pulled closer to him once more. It was like I'd become his sleeping bolster for him to calm down. Surprisingly, it was also calming me down to sleep in his warmth. He put me in my place, where I belonged, under the blanket of his hug.

In the morning, we woke up early. It was both our doctor's appointments. I cooked scrambled eggs and toast for our breakfast. I got some red beans from the warmer.

We had our first meal at the restaurant. It was funny to see him smile, since I wasn't used to seeing it. He took his coffee black, no milk or sugar. He didn't add any salt or pepper to his eggs, either. It was something new I needed to keep in mind about him. Coffee, plain. Eggs, plain.

He left the restaurant first since his health exam had more items to be done. I took a cleaning cloth to our place after breakfast. I cleaned the dining table in our quarter before I took a shower this morning.

12

Road to Recovery

Mandy

Max was on the treadmill when I entered the medical centre. He had straps and wires on his bare chest and wrist. Our eyes connected for a few seconds, but he didn't slow down his running pace. It was good; he needed to focus on what he was doing. And I wanted him to succeed in his training.

The nurse told me to wait in the chair because the doctor was still monitoring Max. It made me wonder how long he had been running. Was it always this challenging for every onboarding shadow-worker?

After a while, the doctor came to check my wound with a nurse. "It's going well so far, but you need to keep it dry. I'll prescribe the ointment to be applied twice a day. Keep it light, not too much."

"I will, doctor. Is there anything that I can or cannot eat?"

"For now, try not to have too much seafood. Just until the wound fully heals. Is there anything else you'd like to ask?"

"Um, how is my husband doing? With his test?"

"That one, I cannot answer. He's your husband, but at the same time, he is a trainee."

"I understand."

"But I can tell you to support him during his training."

"That one, I can do for sure." I left the centre, slowing down my walking pace when passing Max. On my way out, our eyes were connected one more time. This time, he winked at me as if he told me that he was all right. I couldn't see his face because of the oxygen mask he was wearing.

"How long does he need to run?"

I had been in there quite a while. He had been on the treadmill since the time I arrived and was still on it when I left. If only I knew that it would be the last time I saw him for the rest of the day.

I explored different deck levels the entire day. It was nice to talk with the ship crew. They told me to first visit the farm and green houses since they needed some help with picking the eggs and harvesting the fruit.

The crew was giving a curtsy to a lady. She looked so beautiful and elegant with her black hair, even with the pale skin that she had.

Giving a curtsy, I said to her, "Milady."

"The newlywed is working already? How's the honeymoon phase for you two?"

"Quite busy, Milady. He's still in his training."

"Did they assign you here to work?"

"Oh, no. I came here by myself. I need to keep myself occupied during the day. Although I sent my application to CID yesterday."

"Good, then. My husband is good with plants; I'm not. They usually die in my hands. But it's nice to harvest them. It can be quite soothing if you ask me. I just gave up on growing them."

"I'm sure they understood your kind intention in growing them. Neither can I keep even a cactus alive."

"Haha. I guess we're not made for plants. Tell me, Mandy, what do you like doing in your alone time?"

"I, um, am fond of reading, Milady. You have a wonderful library on Deck 11."

"It's the open one."

"Wait, what? There is more library?"

"Well, if your husband passes his training, he might be shadow-working full time. And if the institution chooses to assign you to the Archive Department, you might have a chance to enter the other library."

"I believe in my husband. And I hope the Archive Department will have an open position for me to fill. I'm looking forward to it. I love burying myself in the pages of books. Um, some sort of escapism for me."

"You've been questioning yourself a lot in your head, haven't you? You've been *umm-ing* too many times already."

"I haven't realised my *umm-ing*, honestly. Although my husband told me for quite some time that I tend to overthink too much in my head, I know that he was right. I just don't know how not to, yet."

"That's wonderful to hear. It means he's been paying close attention to you. I believe he didn't think twice when he jumped to catch you."

I sighed before saying, "I don't feel like I deserve him sometimes. He always catches me from falling apart and builds me back together again, even before we get married."

"Not every man is willing to take the leap of faith for his woman. My husband once decided to take the leap. It was a long time ago. I still don't feel like deserving him to this day."

"From what you told me, I believe he's been a good husband for you, Milady."

"Indeed, he is."

I returned to our place near sunset. I was thinking about what Milady said while taking a shower. It was so late that Max hadn't returned from training.

Remembering what Max told me, I ate without him, even though I didn't feel like having any. I didn't eat much, but enough to keep me from fainting.

It was around midnight when I went out to the pantry to stock some first aid supplies and medicines. I was restless the entire night. Even when I fell asleep, I kept waking up almost every hour. I didn't double lock the door in case Max returned.

13

Heated

Mandy

In the morning, I woke up only to find his bedside empty. There was a yoga class at the gym. I found out that it was open to any ship crew and shadow-workers who wanted to join.

Taking a shower after yoga and washing my hair were the only ways to cool down my head. I wasn't sure if Max was all right. I tried to keep myself busy waiting for Max.

I had my lunch alone on Deck 3. They served pasta today. After that, I decided to wash our clothes. I paused, holding the last shirt he wore in my hand. I didn't know why my stomach hurt. We hadn't had sex yet, so I couldn't be pregnant.

"We usually keep that one, the last shirt our spouse wore before going to work, just in case. But no, you're not alone. Hang in there, sister," said a ship crew. He left the laundrette after that, not even waiting for my response.

I kept the shirt unwashed. I washed and dried the other clothes. "Should I ask anyone about Max?" Even if I asked anyone, I didn't know who to ask.

After ironing the clothes, I returned to our place. I hadn't put any of our clothes in the wardrobe yet. Instead, I went to have tea earlier in the restaurant and ate as fast as I could. So when Max returned, he would find me inside.

The door opened when I was putting the clothes in the wardrobe. His clothes looked wet at some point but dried out while he was wearing them. "You okay, princess?"

"Why wouldn't I be all right?"

He finger-combed his damp hair, saying, "Did you eat yet?"

"I did, as you told me." I pulled a t-shirt, underpants, and track pants for when he was done showering.

"And when I didn't come home yesterday..." he paused to take off his shirt. "Did you eat?" He sat down, taking off his shoes.

"I did." Our skin touched one another when he was taking off his shirt and socks. I touched his face and neck and placed the back of my hand on his forehead. I felt his warmth, but it was warmer than usual.

"Good. You started to listen to me." He took off his trousers and underpants, facing the bathroom. "I'm gonna take a shower."

"You have a fever. Careful, not too long in the shower."

"Oh, it'll be long if you decide to join me in there."

"Max, it's not funny. I shall get you something to eat so you can take the medicine. I stocked them yesterday, just in case."

He chuckled and said, "No worries, I'll be all right."

"Obviously, it isn't the time for me to listen to you."

In the shared kitchen, I cooked chicken cream soup for him. I took some bread before returning to our place. Max was already lying in bed when I came in. His fever was higher than before.

"Max, wake up. You need to eat before going to sleep. I made some soup. Come on, just a bit."

"You really didn't have to." He sat up in bed. After scooping up the first one, he said, "It's delicious, princess."

Although I didn't know how it really tasted, he continued to eat. "Oh, Max. The fever is getting higher."

He took the last piece of bread I held in my hand. He used it to scoop the last drop of the soup from the container.

"I shall get the medicine for you. No arguing."

He drank the hot tea and took the medicine I gave him. "Just leave them there. I'll put them out in the morning. Come here."

I locked the door and turned the lights off. The small desk light should be enough for him to see me taking off my clothes. Wearing only a bra and knickers, I climbed up our bed. Laying down at my side of the bed, I said to him, "You should come here."

He laid his head on my chest. He took a deep breath and exhaled in relief. "Thanks for the cooking. Sorry, I got held up last night. You didn't sleep, did you?"

Keeping our skin to skin, I rubbed his back and ran my finger through his hair strains. "I fell asleep, but you shouldn't worry about me. I think you should be focusing on your training."

I kept rubbing and scratching his back and head. I felt his breathing calmer.

"Yes, princess?"

"I didn't say anything."

"Oh, I thought you called me. You squeezed the back of my neck twice. Long squeezes."

"I don't understand. What does it mean?"

"We do these things, signalling at work. Sometimes with taps, squeezes, or even blinks. Two dashes, Morse code for M."

"Good thing you told me. Besides, both our names start with M. Now I know if you're calling me out there. Like this?" I squeezed his arm twice, a long squeeze each.

"Yeah, like that. I might also call you like this." He tapped me twice, with a long pressure each time. "Or like this." His thumb rubbed my skin twice, with a long stroke each time.

"Hmm... I think I like it. You should get some rest."

And those two dashes became another one of our things. I kept hugging and rubbing him until he was asleep before I let myself go into the depths of the night.

14

Calming Water

Mandy

He was sweating on my chest and stomach when I woke up. Fortunately, his temperature had gone down. His morning wood was only layers away from my thigh.

I tried not to move him or wake him up. If only I could install a tap at my folds, because it was only layers of my knickers holding the leakage. I felt his thumb rub in two long strokes.

"Your heartbeat's racing, princess." He opened his eyes, but he didn't move away from me.

"Oh, um, I'm sorry I woke you up. You were hot last night. But much cooler now. How are you feeling?" I kept holding him in my arms.

"So... I'm cool now? But last night, I was hot. I'm lost. Like, which one do you want?" He chuckled while rubbing my arm. He lifted my thighs so they could hold onto his waist.

"I'm glad you came back last night. I sort of missed my blanket."

"Got it. Gotta be hot. My sleeping bolster tends to get her feet cold at night."

"So that's why I mostly hesitate. I get cold feet easily." I wanted to keep him like this the entire day if I had a say.

He raised his head when there was a sliding sound on the floor. He lifted himself off of me to get it. Reading it, he smiled and then looked at me. "It's for 'Mrs. Mandalina Saint,' from the Archive Department," he said.

"What is it with that face?"

He handed me the envelope. "Nothing, just reading my last name following your first."

"Well, you need to get used to it. Ugh, did I get a job?"

"I dunno. Open it." He left me to use the loo.

While I kept staring at the envelope, I heard him washing his hands and face inside the bathroom. "Max, I'm scared. What if they don't accept me?"

I crawled towards him and sat on my knees at the edge of the bed. I looked up at him. "What if I don't get a job here? What do I do?"

He ran his fingers through my hair, then held the back of my head. His towering, built up body in front of me turned my leakage into a river of arousal.

"Let me see it." He showed me the front side of the envelope while massaging my head. "See that? It says, 'Mrs. Saint.' Let me take care of my wife."

"You should open it." I waited in silence while he read it.

"You got an offer as the archiving crew. It says that you need to report to the library on Deck 11."

"I got an offer?" I gasped before reading the letter. After jumping onto him, I hugged him tightly.

"Well, you're still a probie for two duty rotations. So you'll be learning a lot on the job."

I looked him straight in the eyes. "I will do my best, Max. I promise."

"You'd better do, princess."

"Oh, I need to take a shower and go to the library. Wait. Do I cook first or take a shower first?" I paused, watching him shrug. "Okay, I'll take a shower first."

There was a part of me that hoped that Max would barge in and join me in the shower. My body froze when I saw the shadow of his footsteps through the door threshold. My heartbeat raced as he stood there for a few seconds, but then I heard him opening the wardrobe.

He didn't come in to join me. Instead, he opened the bathroom door a little bit. His hand slipped between the gaps, carrying a hanger. He put them on the hook inside the bathroom. He prepared my shirt, trousers, bra, and knickers. They were hung together. After he closed the door again, I continued showering.

He had been taking care of me, but I wondered if he considered our marriage a real one. He hadn't yet touched me in bed. He made me wonder if he ever found me attractive at all. We hugged while sleeping, but nothing more than that.

"Thanks for, um, preparing my clothes."

"You look nice." And then he went to take his shower while I prepared his shirt in turn.

In the kitchen, I cooked a frittata for us. It was simple and easy because I needed to go to the library after breakfast.

***

Max

I should have barged in when she was showering. I should have taken her in the most senseless way possible.

She probably had no idea what she had done to me. The moment she was down to her underwear last night, all I could think about doing was ripping them off and having her completely naked. The entire night, I rested my head in between her breasts, only inches away from sucking her nipples.

I woke up to smell her arousal leaking out of her pussy and pooling in her panties. That scent of hers fucked my mind. Her heart raced as if she were catching her breath when I finally made her come.

While holding my cock in my fist, I recalled every chance I missed. That moment when she crawled towards me earlier. The way she sat in front of me. She looked up at me, just like she was my good pet, waiting for my cock as a treat.

When I held the back of her head in my hands, it was only one pull away from exposing her neck. I should have shoved my cock down her throat. I pumped my cock with the image of her swallowing me.

It must had felt good to feel her gagging and see her tears run down her beautiful face. Imagining her hollowed cheeks when she sucked my girth, I stroked myself harder. It could have been so satisfying to empty my balls down her throat instead of wasting my cum on my hand in the shower like this. She deserved every drop of my cum; my hand did not.

She was my wife; that was how I saw her. I wasn't sure how she saw me, especially with these swellings and bruises. It seemed like she was taking care of me. But I couldn't force her to see me as her husband. She never expressed her agreement with me branding her as my wife; that was on me. That was *my* decision to take her as my wife. I'd keep standing by the decision I made.

Mandy had started to cook for me since we got here. She rarely cooked in the past, let alone cooked for me.

"Here's your coffee. I cooked a frittata for us."

"I appreciate it, princess." I took my first bite. "It's delicious. You know, you can cook it however you like it, maybe adding salt."

She pouted her lips, looking down at her plate. "I'm trying here, Max."

I rubbed my thumb on her hand, making two long strokes. "Just because I rarely use salt doesn't mean you need to cater everything to me. I'll take anything you give me. Trust me, the stray dog won't complain."

"You're no longer a stray dog." She was right; I had a home now. Her.

"Anyway, I took the medicine from the pantry. Just in case you'd be stubbornly saying, 'Oh, I'll be alright.' Here it is; no excuses. You'll take one before going for training today."

She took the flatware to the dishwasher after we finished. I felt like she was returning to our table only to watch me swallow the medicine. She was cute this way, if you asked me.

"Are you sure I look alright?"

"No, you're not. You look beautiful as always." I watched her cheeks blush upon hearing my words. "You got this. You got college degrees, so it'll be a piece of cake for you."

"You think so, Max?"

"Of course, I do."

I watched her leave the restaurant before I went to my training. I never knew that it would be my last time seeing her for the next week or two. If I knew, I would have dragged her to bed and handled her the way she deserved it.

15

Wisdom of Knowledge

Mandy

Even though he wasn't as showing and warm as I'd like to see him, I felt his support for me. I could have hugged Max before leaving the restaurant. I should have.

I wanted it to be real at this point. Us. Our marriage. I meant it when I said that he was no longer a stray dog. He had a home now, with me. That was, if he chose to build it with me.

"Hi. I'm Sofia. How can I help you?"

"Yes, I'm Mandy. I received this letter in my quarter."

"Ah, you are the new recruit. Please, come inside." She led me to her office. "You will be on probation for two consecutive duty rotations. We have many who fled their origins, so we don't conduct the recruitment phase the way most companies do. You and your husband still have to pass probation. Fortunately, you came at the same time."

"Is there anything that you'd like to ask about me?"

"It seems like you like books. Why do you like reading?"

"It's different from time to time. When I read fiction, it's sort of like escaping the real world. But for nonfiction, it was like a puzzle for me. To find the missing pieces."

"Do you always accomplish your TBR?"

"Not all the time; it's different each year. In some years, I read more. But some other years, I was short behind."

"In the beginning, you'll do a clerical job. You are to document the rotation of books, manage shelves, and display arrangements. But from time to time, you need to do research on which books are best-selling and popular."

"May I ask if this is mainly a library or a bookstore?"

"Here on Deck 11, we're hybrid between the two functions. The one on Deck 10 is different. They have more variables to manage since they're restricted to shadow-workers and ship crew. During probation, you are limited to Deck 11. Your husband can enter the library on Deck 10 under supervision."

"Understood."

"So, here is your agreement draft. You can read and learn through the pages for a few days. If you choose to accept the agreement, you will sign it at the CID. If you choose not to accept, you need to inform them as well, so they can offer you another position in another department. Is there anything you'd like to ask me?"

"I think I can see myself here, buried in an ocean of books."

"You haven't seen the salary page yet."

"But I love the smell of books."

"I know, right? They smell different than other things in life."

I spent some time in the library reading the draft. They had dictionaries and references for me to see if there was something in the draft that I wasn't sure about.

Sofia found it funny that I asked about how to do the job and actually tried to do the job without signing the agreement first. Guests scattering the books off their shelves bothered me, especially when they decided not to buy them. She asked more about me in the library than in the interview we did earlier, which by far made it the best interview I ever did.

I couldn't wait to tell Max about the interview. Even though I couldn't read him sometimes, I needed to see his face. It was important for me to know if he was proud of me in any way. Before going to the supplies room on Deck 7, I took a lunch break on Deck 11.

One journal and a couple of pens should be enough for me to start the job. Except it turned out that it wasn't. There were plenty of colourful pens, highlighters, and colour pencils in there. Not to mention different types of journals and notebooks. Slava made me wonder what the institution was truly like. Everything they provided wasn't only about necessities but also preferences or even hobbies. What kind of company gave these things to their crews? Once I got my stationery, I returned to the library.

On their computer, I searched for recipes. They stored different types of pasta in the pantry. Pastina would be perfect for tea; it was said to be an Italian penicillin.

This was my initial plan. To check all the ingredients and cook it later when Max returned, except he never did tonight. I waited for him long enough before deciding to eat by myself. What they cooked in the kitchen tonight was enough for tea.

16

Taken

Mandy

Max had not returned for two days now. So, I decided to take the job offer at the library. That way, I could ask about Max when I signed the agreement at CID.

"You can ask the equipment crew for uniforms and other things that you'd need for the job. Those uniforms are bulletproof; nevertheless, you need to attend self-defence classes. Fortunately, you're the wife of someone with such skills, so you two can practise together. Here is the list of your benefits and classes that we open for shadow-workers and crew."

"I can join any of these classes for free?"

"Yes, they are for free. There is a reason why we're named the Capital and Investing Department. Because it *is* an investment to train and upgrade our human resources."

"I've heard that your department manages animals and plants, too."

"We do. It's related directly to what we consume. Just because we're floating doesn't mean that we can't provide natural livestock and plants. Especially for shadow-workers, they need to stay fit for the job. You take care of your husband; he can't get sick during projects."

"Speaking of my husband, he was sick the night before he went back to training. May I know if he's all right? It's been a few days."

"He didn't get so much action going when he was your bodyguard, did he?" She looked at her laptop after she asked me the question.

I chuckled and said, "No, he didn't. It was only me and the house for about a half year."

"I will ask the Health Department because I haven't gotten any notice of inpatients. I assume that it was his body making some adjustments. He was, well, let's say, *intense* in his previous career. But then he loosened up while working with you. Now he's in the state of reactivating his muscle memories."

"Am I allowed to know what he would need for his work? Um, training, for now. I mean, not details, but simple things like what he can eat or cannot eat. Since I'll be cooking a lot for him."

"Firstly, you need to wait for him to return. Secondly, you can ask him about his meal plan when he was in the Army. Thirdly, you need to ask him if he needs some adjustments for shadow-working. Lastly," she paused. She watched me write notes in my journal. "And this is foremost important. You can cook for him a lot, but not too much. He cannot have a dad-bod when working with us. Wives do that too much sometimes."

We laughed at what she said. It was a nice way of telling me not to worry about Max. She had a point.

After receiving my uniforms, I washed them clean, along with other dirty clothes. I also washed our bedsheet so Max would sleep on the fresh one when he returned.

The next morning, I started my job in the library after breakfast. They gave me eight hours of work a day, with an hour of break in between. My schedule during a duty rotation was five days of work and one day off after. The more senior crew had three days of work and one day off after.

Because I was the newest crew member in the department, I got my lunch after one of the crew members returned. Mia came to the library at lunchtime. She and I had our lunch on Deck 9, far away from other archive crew members.

"So, how's your first day of work?"

"It was massive. I've never seen anything like this library before. Modern, but still has the classic touch. Classic, but not old. Do you know what I mean?"

"Well, congrats on your new job. Then why the fuck are you looking like shit?"

"Hhh... you know how massive they are, and I'm short compared to the shelves. It's not that I'm complaining. I'm grateful for even having a job without carrying any documents. I need to figure out a better way to put the bigger books on the higher shelves."

"Really? The shelves are *massive*, you said? You know that it isn't what I was talking about. Don't fool me as if I just know you for five minutes."

"What do you want me to say, Mia? I don't know about this side of the world. When I signed the crew agreement, the CID crew said something like, 'He was intense in the Army.' I didn't know what that meant. Although he can be annoying sometimes, he's always watching my back."

"Oh, Mandy. He's not the first ex-military member to join the institution, but you're my friend. It's hard to see you like this."

"Those books and shelves sort of help me."

"Mandy, can I ask you something?"

"Yes, I think I want it to be real. The word is 'want,' but I don't know if he wants it, too. I know what you were about to ask."

"Did he ever hurt you?"

"No, he didn't. He's rather surprisingly sweet to me. In a flat, unreadable way."

"Pfft, I'm not sure men with this tough type of job can ever be sweet. If you know what I mean," she said with a wink. She watched my facial reaction, waiting for me to talk more.

"What?"

She was gasping. "I cannot believe you two haven't..." She looked around and whispered, "You haven't fucked?"

I shook my head at her.

"Mandy, I'm saying this as your friend. You've been through a lot with your mum. I was there. Don't lie to me by saying it was nothing."

"Moving to London while my parents got divorced wasn't easy. Especially when their accounts were frozen. But it was necessary, Mia. We wouldn't have bumped into each other if I didn't work mopping that coffeeshop."

"But it was great you got promoted to become a barista. I got lots of coffee from your practice batch. Haha." She paused before continuing the reminiscence, "It was your mum's death that hit you hard, wasn't it?"

"Looking back, I wonder if mum giving up had unconsciously planted some weird thoughts in my head. I had tried to avoid the thought, but eventually, I jumped off that day."

"I know you would. It was almost like I could see you jumping off that cliff, even before you actually did it. That was why I signalled him."

"Signalled him how? What do you mean? He was far away from me. Even further from you."

"Do you remember hearing the ship's horn?"

"I do. It was long that morning. I thought you were doing those weird honking like the truck drivers."

"He got my broadcast. When you walked backwards from that cliff, CQD. Come Quick Danger. He got the heads up right away. I saw him through my bins. Not only him, but all the shadow-workers were on alert at that time."

"Ugh, I'm feeling awful. Did they get troubled because of me? Did you?"

"No, because when I saw you pausing before running, I broadcasted MX CLF."

"Max cliff?"

"I'm a captain first, but I'm also your friend, Mandy." She held my hand in hers. "You can ask him about this marriage thing you have when he returns. But from what I saw that morning, as soon as he got my message, he threw your tumbler. He just ran towards you. You know, he didn't stop before jumping to get you. Straight jump."

"So I can't be mad at him for spilling my coffee, can I? I loved that tumbler."

"Unbelievable."

For more than a week, Max hadn't returned. I kept my head down at work. I started working in time but finished late. It was better to keep me busy; my day off became torture for me.

17

Hanging to Stall

Max

"One more day. Floret, I know you're closer to the Divine than me. Tell the Creator that I need another day. Not for me, but for my wife. Please. I'd live for her."

I never had training in the military that felt so fucking real as the training I got here. Maybe they had one for another different branch. And holy fuck, they were doing it while wearing those damn suits? Class. But it got me thinking about how I'd do that if I got accepted here.

Guarding Mandy was already itching me out with the smart-casual outfit. I could only imagine how I'd be scratching here and there while wearing those suits. I wondered what my wife would think when I wore one of those suits. Would she see me differently? Would it make her want to make us real and make it work?

Counting days and nights was already useless. There were only here and now. They had hung me upside down since then.

"*I just need another day. Another day until I see Mandy again.*" That was what I kept saying in my head for the past week or two.

Mia, Captain Phinnisee just came in. Mandy met her when she was in college. They had known each other long enough for her to read Mandy from a distance and in an instant. She was the one who warned me about Mandy taking her jump that morning.

"What did you do?"

I hadn't felt any movement for a while. This ship had been drifting away from her course. "I did what I did. Which one of my doing are we talking about again?"

She took off her uniform and put it aside.

"Ooo, the captain wants a piece. Do you do this often? Sharing men between friends kinda stuff?"

She hit me all right. "What have you done to my ship?"

"Though, I never thought the orphan would be joining the captain's cunt sharing club. It used to be only with the brothers, no? Though I'm glad the orphan joined the club, less stray dogs on the street."

Another hit landed on me. "Let me ask you one more time. What have you done to my ship?"

"Since when she became your ship? Did you get a share of the institution? That's a lotta sharing goin' on in your life, Captain."

She landed another hit on me. "Let me be clear. If you mess up with the ship, we can get plenty of engineers to fix her. But if you dare to mess with my friend, it won't be the Angel of Death coming your way. I'm going to rip your balls off and shove them down your throat. 'Death by the balls' can't be glorious, innit?"

"No, it won't. But you won't get to touch my balls, either. They're your friend's property."

"We're not done yet." She put her uniform back on.

She was heading out of the room when I said, "She's my wife, Mia. Let her think that I'm in training here. Clearly, I'm just stalling."

She held the door half open. "What did you just say?" She closed the door again and walked towards me.

"Stalling for what?"

"As I said, she is my wife. I can take the hit. But if any of you dare to touch my wife, Imma rip off what you've been keeping in the womb before shattering this ship apart. But since you're Mandy's friend, I'll let you watch Slava sink, Captain."

Their Great One entered the room and closed the door behind him. "Captain, you might want to tuck in your uniform first."

"My Great One." The captain gave him a curtsy before heading to the corner of the room.

I closed my eyes to keep myself away. Then I felt my hanging body being turned the other way.

"Let's give the captain some decency, shall we?"

"I appreciate that, Sir. Sir? Angel? What am I supposed to call you? Like, I don't know your name, really."

"Samael. But different people from different places call me by different names. It's rather annoying to track down all those names, if you ask me."

"No fucking way. You're kidding me, right? And your wife's the Lilith? Wait, I thought you were chained somewhere."

He chuckled at my words. "Rereading the scriptures might be helpful for you, if I may suggest."

"Scriptures from which belief do I reread first? I mean, different beliefs said different things about you."

"That's my point. Do you know what I mean?"

Mia came back to us. "Hey, focus!"

"I am, Captain. I haven't lost my focus, can you see?"

Their Great One asked, "So what do you want? Any request for exchange of some kind?"

"What do you mean? I'm not requesting anything."

"Then what is it with dismantling my ship if you don't have any requests?"

I couldn't help but laugh at their frustration with me. Kinda funny to watch, if you ask me. "Australia was a decoy, no? So I was only showing you that your systems have flaws. Yo, for real, I didn't bring anything with me, but I *could* stop your ship just like that. Imagine those motherfuckers with massive artillery coming for a war with you. And I'm supposed to trust you with my wife when I'm working?"

He continued to ask, "And you are saying?"

"Look, I know those shadow-workers have the skills. That, I can tell. I can trust them with my life if I choose to work with y'all. With the flaws in your systems, I ain't trusting you with my wife. If you want me to work with you, it could be a deal breaker. Other than that, I'm just stalling."

"Oh, this youngling! I'd rather not say that you might be right. But you got a point."

"See, I'm not that hard to read." Even though my wrists were tied behind my back, I tried to bend forward. Tucking inside with my core, my hands could reach the ropes that hung me from the ceiling.

"With two rotations, there's gonna be 23 weeks left or so. I still have time to think about alternatives. I'll get whatever is available on the ground if I choose *not* to work with you. In the meantime, my wife gets a bed to sleep on and three square meals a day. This so-called training is fair enough."

"Public service announcement, Mandy accepted the job offer in the library. She shall be all right on her own."

"Yeah, good luck telling her that. She overthinks everything. You know, when she's reading but isn't really reading. Her mind's not really all there. She questions herself a *lot*." I held the ropes with my tied hands and kicked the ceiling upside down.

"I got my suspicions about Slava way back when. But I didn't report everything I saw, no?" I kept kicking the ceiling again until finally, it crumbled down. Then I hit the cold floor.

When I was trying to stand up, a punch landed on me. Their Great One surely had different powers than others. Since that hit, all I saw next was blackness and nothingness.

18

Home

Mandy

When Mia came to the library, I was still doing the decorations for the book display. "Ooh, you're sweating, darling."

"You should finish your work on time. Trust me."

I watched her leave the library without saying anything else. There were about twenty minutes left for me to clock out. It was about finishing every detail in the decorations as neatly as I could in a short amount of time.

It must be Max that she was talking about. I hoped he was all right, but having him return to me would be enough. It had been too long without hearing any news about him.

My eagle eyes watched the clock ticking; I waited near Sofia's office. When the needle reached 12, I knocked on her door to say goodbye.

As I was excited about seeing Max, I walked as fast as I could without bumping anyone. At the same time, I was anxious about how he was.

When I reached the aisle on Deck 3, I sped up my walk. There, I saw Max unconscious, being carried by two shadow-workers from the other side of the aisle. I was almost running at this point. Once I opened the door to our place, those shadow-workers threw him on the floor inside.

"He insisted on being brought to the missus. He needs to join the class the day after tomorrow."

Nodding without saying anything should be enough. I wasn't sure whether I should thank them or slap them across the face.

Once they left, I rolled Max over to see how bad he was. "Oh, Max. I'm glad you're home." I took a damp cloth to wipe his swollen and bruised face. Gently, because I didn't want to hurt him more than he already did. Someone was knocking on the door.

"It's not my place to ask, but I saw them bringing your man here. I figured I'd bring this stuff. Then you'll be here when he wakes up. If you two need a hand, I'm five quarters from here, starboard."

"I appreciate your help. I couldn't thank you enough." There were ice packs, salt, washing clothes, painkillers, packs of crackers, and two packs of fresh sandwiches in the bucket.

Max was taller and heavier than me, so rolling his body was as much as I could do while cleaning him. I couldn't even focus on the muscles in his upper body or on his cock in the underpants. His wounds and bruises clouded all of them.

Late at night, I felt his stroking call. "That's it. It's gotten into your subconscious, no? I'll teach you some Morse one day. The basics, so you can call for help in case I'm not around."

"I'd love to learn it after *this* mess is healed."

He moved his head away from resting on my thigh. After he folded my legs, he crawled on his stomach towards my inner thighs. "Hmmh, this smells like home," he said while sniffing my folds. He slept so close to my pussy for the entire night, hugging my hips.

***

I woke up in the morning to find him staring at me. "Good morning."

"Good morning, princess. I heard you got the job. How's your first week?"

Sleeping down on the floor in a sitting position had its own souvenirs for the muscles. I was stretching my body as far as I could. "I should be the one asking how you are, Max."

"Owh, my princess's hurting. No worries. Tonight, you'll sleep in a suite. We're moving up."

"Could you please stop it? Really? Asking if I'm hurt sleeping on the floor while you're obviously more hurt because of me? So, yeah, my first week at work was all right." I sighed heavily. "I need to use the loo."

The bathroom was a better way, rather than letting my pooling tears fall in front of him. Milady was right about her husband. It felt like I didn't deserve someone like Max.

"Couldn't help it. I'm starving." He was eating the sandwich on the table when I got out of the bathroom. "I miss your cooking, by the way. Did you eat last night?"

"They're from the neighbour. He said that he saw you being brought here. So he gave us this stuff and something to eat. We should thank him later."

"Yeah, we should. Come here, princess." He pulled me to sit on his lap, although I knew that they were hurt. "Really, I'm asking you. Are you all right?"

"No. I miss my blanket. I'm glad you're here, Max. I do."

"Me, too, princess. How about you make us some breakfast and I take a shower? Really, I'm still hungry. You make it the way you like it, yeah?"

"After breakfast, you will go to see the doctor. Last night, they told me that you insisted on being brought here. Do we have a deal?"

"I've got my own nurse here. She's cute when she's worried. But okay, if you insist."

19

Shattered

Max

Mandy was lying on the couch, not in our bed. I tucked myself under the blanket beside her and placed her head on my arm.

"Max, why are you here? You should be sleeping in bed."

"The question is, why are you here, princess?"

"We got upgraded to this suite because you passed the training. You deserve the bed. I do a library job, so I'm supposed to continue living in the quarter."

"I deserve to sleep with my wife. Unless I'm at work, I might be crashing on someone's couch. Or even sleeping on the street like a stray dog I used to."

She sighed before saying, "Max, I appreciate what you've done for us. But honestly, I don't even know if this marriage is real. We've never talked about it. I mean, us."

"We're talking about us right now. I meant it when I branded you as my wife. At least it's been real for me." I started to run my fingers through her smooth hair. "Look, I know I'm not good at this relationship thing. It's been a long time since I've been in one."

"But if you said that it's real, then why haven't you touched me? I thought the marriage was fake and, um, that you don't want me."

"Ugh. You have no idea how many seeds I've spilt in the shower. All thinking about you. Of course, I want you."

"You what? Max, since when?"

"Since long before we left." I kissed her lips gently. Our first proper kiss, millions to go. "Marrying you was an easy choice for me. I saw an opportunity, and I took it."

"Remember when we were in the car with my father? I said that you could marry me. I meant it. All this time, it's been real for me, too."

"Yes, I remember." I gave her another kiss. "And I remember you telling me to find you in another life. Then you'd marry me in that life."

"And this is that life." That gaze she was giving me surely melted what's been inside my chest but hardened my cock in an instant.

"What? You're not pregnant already, are you? I thought you were on pills."

She gasped. "How did you know I was on pills?"

"You had no problem handing me other lists of supplies back then, unless that every first week of the month visit to the drugstore. For that one, you needed to get them yourself. But I haven't seen any pills since we got here. Whose idea were the condoms?"

"They were from the first day we got here. The doctor asked me if I was on birth control and told me that the OBGYN was available the next morning. But I told him that I needed to talk with you first. Then he gave them to me while lightly saying something like, 'This should fit your husband.' I mean, how would I know?"

"Oh, you're about to find out. *That one*, I can guarantee. But hell no, I ain't using no condoms with you. You're my wife. Latino have big families. Some of us, but not all. And I want a big family, too. With you, *if* you want it."

She nodded in the cutest way I had ever seen her. "I'd love to have a big family with you. Please." That *'please'* made my cock fight to be liberated from my pants.

My lips started kissing and lapping hers. My hand was on auto, slipping under her t-shirt to her perky breasts. Those nipples were screaming to be sucked. "Tell me. Have you ever thought of me?"

"Of course I have. But I didn't feel like touching myself. I needed your scent, your voice, and your touch."

"And what about when you were with those princes? Were you thinking about me?"

"It was you who touched me, never them. I felt that you were with me on those nights."

"I know you're not lying. Those nights when I knew you were with them, I could almost hear you calling my name. Your voice woke me up many times." I traced down to her neck.

"Oh, Max... I was calling for you on those nights. To save me from them, kidnap me, even. It sounds odd, but I was."

When I licked her from the collarbone to her ear, the hair on her arms suddenly rose. "Yeah, I heard you."

"Mmh... please, Max. I'm yours already."

"That's right, you're mine. And I'm telling you to slip your hand inside your panties. Your fingers will find my pussy down there. You heard me right, it's mine."

"Max, you should be the one touching me. Please don't do this to me." She did as I said anyway.

I lifted her t-shirt, exposing her breasts. "Squeeze my breasts with the other hand. They're my breasts now. One by one. Eyes on me. You need to see who owns this princess."

With my hand on her throat, I gave her the perfect collar. "Now play with those nipples and clit at the same time. No stopping unless I say so."

She let out a moan from her pink lips. She bit her bottom lip before letting out another moan. I couldn't wait to kiss her other lips.

"What a beautiful, obedient slut wife I got here. Get a finger inside... Keep circling the clit with your thumb." Her moans could have made me lift her and throw her onto our bed. But I needed to hold myself back. This princess needed to learn how to beg first.

"You want me inside you tonight?"

"Mmm... hmm."

"Then get another finger inside you." Fuck, I needed to get her nipples pierced. "Also pinch those nipples for me."

"Max, please. I need you." Her moaning sound became more like a craving.

"Tell me how you feel."

"Desperate, mmh... for you to take me. Please, Sir."

"That's more like it. Desperately begging. Let me see how wet you are."

Those fingers of hers were soaked with her needs. I held her wrist to suck clean each of her fingers. "Oh, you taste so good. From now on, I want my pussy to be soaking wet every time I come home. If you don't get wet, you need to make it ready for me. But you're not allowed to come. *I* tell you when you can come. Understood?"

"Understood, Sir."

I carried her to our bed. Her clothes were no longer covering her. For a moment, I just stood there, watching her naked body. "You're so beautiful."

"Please," she whimpered. With her legs spreading, she showed her glistening pussy.

Kissing her lips, I sucked every breath out of her mouth. "Every breath of air you take is mine. Never forget who owns you." I sucked her nipple while my fingers pinched the other one.

She ran her fingers through my hair. She kissed my head while I was devouring her breasts—my breasts. She let out a moan when I bit her nipple.

"These are mine. And I want them pierced. I'll do it myself if I have to."

"This pussy also belongs to you, Sir. Do you want it pierced, too?"

I moved down to widen her folds. "Yes, right here. I want my pussy pierced right here." I sucked every drop of her wetness before thrusting two fingers into her.

She whimpered again, "Max, please, I'm close." Her moan sang the most beautiful song I hadn't heard in a long time.

I felt her clenching my fingers while I kept savoring her clit. "Who says I only want one? I want you to come over and over until I tell you to stop." I added another finger to ready her for me.

She ran her fingers through my hair, holding on to me. "Oh, Max." Here she was, my princess, releasing herself into my hand and mouth.

Moving up to kiss her lips, I then showed her my fingers. They were covered with her cum. Her delicious juice just tasted like the most refreshing treat of the summer when I slurped it. "I want all of this from you. Make sure you're serving."

Her lips parted as she watched me lick my fingers clean. Her tears started pooling in her beautiful gray eyes. Then I raced those dropping tears before they fell to the pillow. I licked each of them. "No one is allowed to make you cry but me. Only me when I fuck my slut wife."

***

Mandy

He pulled away from me to take his clothes off. Now I knew what the doctor meant about his size. Seeing those piercings he had, I questioned myself about whether I could take all of him.

"Um, Max. I don't think I—"

"I don't care if you think you can take me or not. When I say you can, it means you will." He lifted me and placed me on his lap. "I'll only treat you like a princess this one time."

"I've never been with anyone with these." This lotus position he put me in should help me adjust. I held his cock and stroked him a few times.

"Hey, hey, hey, you're overthinking it again." He cupped my face to kiss my lips gently. "Look at me. Breathe, princess. You don't need to think. Just do as I say."

I positioned myself to take him in. "Don't let me go. Please don't."

"I won't. Tip's in." He kissed my neck. Then he whispered, "Go on. My pussy's made to fit me."

He knew how to take the lead, as if he were in control of my body and my mind. When he said,

'Breathe,' my nerves instantly calmed. When he said, 'You're overthinking everything again,' the noise inside my head instantly evaporated into thin air.

He held my back while I gravitated towards him. That tongue and those lips were devouring my neck, my shoulder, my breasts, and every part of my body that they could reach to consume. "That's it, princess. I was dead before finding you. Now, bury me inside of you."

Once he was completely inside me, he thrust me up to my hilt. Each step of his ladder ascended me to a higher pleasure. He held me tighter, keeping his word about not letting me go.

"I feel so full and... ooh, Max." I had never gotten this full of someone's thickness. At the same time, I was aching to be filled with more of him.

"Not yet. Not until I fill you with my cum." His thrust became harder with each stroke. He started pulling my hair down, letting my neck be exposed for him to lick. "Shatter for me, princess. I ain't no Saint or knight in shining armour coming to save you. I'm only gonna tear your holes apart."

Just like that, I was torn apart. He released me from the desperation of missing him for weeks. He freed me from uncertainty, allowing me to be kept under his ownership.

He laid me down on our bed. "I'm not done with my slut wife yet." With my legs on his shoulders, he stroked me harder and way deeper.

"Mmh... please. I'm too sensitive. I can't anymore."

Pinching my swollen clit, he said, "Oh, you will for me. I'll keep my promise to tear you apart. Then tear apart for your owner." His thumb then started circling my clit while his strokes got harder into me.

"Sir, I... please—" I whimpered, begging for his mercy. Begging for more. All I got were his merciless strokes, which sent me to scream his name once again.

"Now, you've learnt to be one obedient slut wife. Tell me again, what are you?"

"Your slut, Sir."

"That's right. You're no princess when I fuck you. You're only my slut to use." He thrust a few more strokes before filling me with his warm cum.

20

Lines of Duty

Mandy

He laid in bed beside me, holding my hand. Both of us were recovering from our releases. He kissed my hand and placed it on his chest. His heartbeat was what I deserved to feel. "Come here, princess."

On his chest, I placed my hand. Near his heart, my ear listened to it beating. His kiss on my crown was rather sweet. "I thought I'd lost you in the sea that day. I thought I'd lost you because of me being an idiot."

"Nah, you got me for making a reckless decision. You scared the shit out of me by jumping off that cliff. My heart stopped when I saw you still underwater." He pulled my hand from his chest to kiss my palm. "Don't you ever do that again. I can't lose you, princess. When I say don't, it means you won't. Do you hear me?"

"I won't, Max. I promise." I pulled his hand to kiss the back of his hand.

He chuckled.

"Is there something funny?"

"I've never seen you do it to your father. Others kiss their parents' hands whenever they go out or come in. But not you. You just kissed him on his cheek, but nothing more."

"Excuse me, Sir. You can be my new Daddy if you want. Besides, you're my husband. They don't do that only to parents but to husbands as well."

"Oh, I can be your Daddy now?" He placed my hand on his chest. His rubbing my hand all the way to my forearm calmed me down. "If I'm your Daddy, then what will our kids call me?"

"Possibly, 'bruv.' That'll do it." It was wholesome for us to loosen up like this. Yes, it was us. There was an *us* between me and Max.

I loved screeching and scratching his chest hair, even though it might annoy him. "Can I ask you something?"

"Shoot," he said.

"It sort of scared me when I heard things about your time in the Army."

"Are you scared of me?"

"No. I trust you." After kissing his chest, I said, "Can I ask about your work back then?"

"Okay, before you ask me things about my duty in the past or now, let's set some lines here." He sounded more serious now. "My duty is mine. Those occupational hazards that come with it are mine.

They're never yours. My only duty that you need to watch closely is whether I'm a good husband or not. Sometimes I can't read you when you're having whatever debate in your head."

I giggled, not because of his duty. But I never realised that he paid close attention to me.

"Huh, glad you confirmed that noisy overthinking you have. Anyway, you let me know if I'm being a good husband or not. It's important for us. Can you do that?"

"We have reached an agreement, Sir."

"That 'Sir' got my cock twitching again."

"*He* knows which way home is," I said while cupping his pierced cock. "So I can ask?"

"You can ask anything. I'll answer what I can answer. Some things might be dangerous for you to know. Now, what does my princess want to know so badly? Hmm?"

"You can tell me simple things, like what you were doing in the Army back then. Don't lie to me. From what I heard from those shadow-workers, I could tell that you weren't doing desk jobs."

"I can't do a desk job. My ass hurt from sitting too long." He paused to kiss me. "Back then, I was on a smaller team, not like others. There were—"

My gasp stopped his words from coming out. "So that's why they knew you. Even Mia told me once that they weren't quite sure where you stood. You were in special forces, weren't you? What kind, Max?"

He smirked. "Intelligence." He pulled me in to hug me tighter. He must had endured so many different things and worked on the things that most of us civilians didn't have any clue that those even existed. "After a long time doing it, I got promoted. Not too long before I decided to get out."

He combed my hair and kissed me everywhere. "I'm sorry if I ever got too rough with you. Sometimes I forget how teeny-tiny my princess is. Tell me if it's too much for you. I'll stop."

"But I don't want you to hold back. I need you to be free with me in bed. Or somewhere else." While cupping his face, I took my time in silence. Looking at him straight in the eyes, I said, "Um... Max?"

"Yes, princess?"

"I think I like being married to you."

"Oh, I *know* I like being married to you. You need to start being careful of what you say, though."

"Why? What did I say?"

"You don't remember? The morning you said, 'What am I planning? A honeymoon cruise on Slava? With you? Aaw... so sweet.' Look at where we are. Precisely that. Good thing it was a good thing you said."

"Well, it worked, then. Manifesting the universe thing. Oh, I need to start manifesting mini-Max."

"Yes, do that. I want mini-Max and mini-Mandy, like lots of them." He blanketed me with his warmth the entire night as I surrendered myself to him.

21

Training for Manners

Max

It was weird. I didn't know if it was weird good or weird bad. I never imagined seeing myself in the mirror wearing a suit.

"You will have two suits during your probationary period, one black and one gray. You will get two white shirts and one light blue shirt. These are made with the measurements we took when you came here. We need to measure you once every three months. Quarterly at the least."

"Understood. When do I have to wear this?"

"Every day, unless your assignment says otherwise. The rest of the suits and shirts will be delivered after you pass your training."

"There will be more?"

"Of course, sir. For the basics, we prepare five suits for each shadow-worker. We tailor-made black, gray, navy, dark brown, and tan. For those, we will send half a dozen shirts. With two white shirts, two light blue, one cream, and one light gray. With those, you can have seventy five to eighty styles for projects."

"I've never had that many clothes in my life."

"That is only for either double-breasted or single-breasted. Shadow-workers who wear a single-breasted suit with a waistcoat surely can have many more styles, sir. It might be easier for you to see them as your personalized armor."

The way he said 'sir' was different from when Mandy said it. She said it in a much more vulnerable way, surrendering herself to me. Unless she insisted on something, it became her battleground.

Take this morning, for example. She insisted that I see the doctor again because I was twitching in my sleep. It happened that it was from the accumulation of stress and that I was releasing it when I was in a comfortable state. I couldn't help it; she was comfortable to sleep with. She was my home.

My swellings had been better now. I was worried last night that she might freak out over my scary face. It was nothing like I imagined. I didn't feel like I was having sex with her. More like making love to her. She was the princess I needed to praise. At the same time, I needed to fuck my slut. Mine alone.

My class started half an hour before noon at the restaurant for table manners. From foster homes straight to the barracks, I wouldn't know about table manners.

Sometimes I felt like a stray dog that came from the street. I never knew that cutlery, flatware, and silverware were different for some people. All I did was everything necessary at the time. I guessed table manners were a necessity for shadow-working. The training was clearly something new to me.

Repeatedly listening to the word 'manners' today made me want to train Mandy later on. She'd better get her pussy serving when I saw her.

Opening our suite door, I could smell the food she had cooked for me. "I'm home."

"I'm in the bedroom."

There she was, sitting on her knees on the floor. She was only wearing underwear. "You look great, Sir. How's your training going?" She rose herself up, kneeling in front of me.

"You don't need to worry about my training." I combed her smooth hair. "It's your training you need to focus on."

She bit her bottom lips. "My training, Sir?"

"So far, you're doing great. But I need to continue to train my pet tonight."

"What do you want me to do for you?"

"I can smell your cooking. Prepare the dinner for us." I freshened up in the bathroom. I needed to keep myself together by watching her like that. Otherwise, my cock would be saluting her too early. The box breathing came in handy at a time like this.

She was sitting a few feet in front of the bathroom door. The dinner was served on the table. There were steaks with sautéed veggies and mashed potatoes. She watched me take my first bite. "Do you like it that way?"

"It's delicious. But you haven't eaten any."

"I waited for you."

"Crawl to me." I took a sip of water and watched her on all fours. "What did I say about waiting for me? I don't want you to get sick, but you didn't listen to me."

"I want to eat together with you," she said.

I moved my plate aside and brought her plate closer. I started feeding her while she was sitting on the floor. "Let me know if you're full."

Once I finished feeding her, I continued my dinner. "You can use the bathroom while I'm finishing here. Wait for me in the living room after that. You can choose whatever you want to watch."

"Thank you for feeding me."

After finishing my food, I washed the dishes. She was sitting on the floor, watching a movie. I went to the bathroom and cleaned myself.

"Keep your shit together, Máximo. She's your pet tonight. The pet needs to be trained first. Fuck, I wanna fuck her so bad."

Sitting on the couch, I watched the movie with her. "You can change your seat if you need to." She nodded and started to cling to my leg. I kept playing with her hair and massaging her scalp.

We kept watching the movie for about half an hour, until I couldn't stop my hand from moving down her neck. I slid my hand under her bra, squeezing her breast. I turned off the TV because that distraction was no longer working for me.

"Climb here. Bend over my lap," I said while loosening my tie and undoing my top button.

"What did I say about not delaying meals?" I pulled her panties to the center, exposing her cheeks. "You didn't listen to me tonight."

"But I wanted to wait for you." She let out a moan when I started massaging her ass. "It wasn't that long—"

A spank landed on her ass. "You weren't so obedient, were you?"

"You've been gone for weeks. I've missed you." She received another spank from me. "Mmhh, Sir."

"What do you get when you don't listen to what I say?"

"Punishment. Please, I'm sorry. Mmh…" Her whimper after each spank sounded like she was begging for more.

"That's right." I gave her what she always deserved. "Oh, I like seeing you red like this."

"Sir—" Her own scream cut off what she was saying. She took her punishment so well.

I slid my fingers into her folds, only to find her arousal pooling. "That's my dessert; it's so juicy." I licked my fingers, tasting her. "And it tastes so fucking good."

After unhooking her bra, I took my time rubbing her back. "Who owns this one? Hmm?"

"You do. Please, I've missed you."

"Take off my clothes while I'm sucking those nipples."

***

Mandy

He carried me on his shoulder, just like I weighed as light as a feather. He threw me onto our bed, then rolled me. With his tie, he restrained my wrists together behind me. Not only that, but he took off his belt and tied my arms together.

His arms slid underneath me, lifting my thighs. He made them just like his own personal wingspan. "Come for me. I want more juice for dessert." His tongue lapped along my slit before thrusting inside me. His hungry and thirsty mouth made me come so easily.

"Sir, please. Come home to me." I heard him taking off his shoes and trousers.

He pulled my hair so I could see him. "Remind me to buy a leash for my pet one day."

"Oh, I'd love to wear it for you."

He took me from behind, thrusting his cock inside me in one stroke. "I said that I'd only be gentle yesterday. Yesterday is in the past. From now on, I won't be anymore."

My whimpers could no longer be held back. The ladders he had were ramming into my sensitive spot. With his thickness pushing those ladders against my inner walls, he didn't miss any spots that he needed to reach.

"Seeing you cry like this makes all that pain from getting these piercings worth it."

"Mmh, yes. This is what I need."

"Come for me again. More. That's what I want." His strokes became harder. "That's it. My good pet's getting close again."

"Oh, Sir." My inner walls clenched his cock. That was when he shattered me once again.

He rolled me around to lay on my tied arms and wrists. His cock was inside my tender hole once again. "Imma fill my pussy to the brim if you continue being a good pet. Only if you're good."

His hand cupped my cheeks and traced down to my neck. Slowly, he moved to my breasts. "Oh, so beautiful," he said before slapping both my breasts in turn.

"Hhh... mmh..."

"There. My handprints. These are mine. Only my babies are allowed to have their mouths on these breasts." He started thrusting at me again. Another couple of slaps landed on my breasts. "I'll watch them sucking your milk while having this pussy milking my cock."

"It'll be my honour to carry your babies, Sir. Please fill my womb with your babies."

"Oh, no, no. This womb belongs to me. It's mine, not yours." He lifted my thighs and held them down. Spread them wide. Opened my pussy wider. "Can't wait to fuck you when your swollen belly grows my baby in it."

His wild strokes eased down when I felt his warmth filling me. "I disagree, princess. It'll be my honour." He closed the gap between my thighs. Lifting me from the bed, he rolled his body along with me.

My body laid on top of him while our stomachs were attached together. He freed my wrists from his tie and my arms from his belt. "Please tell me if I've gone too far with you."

I loved how the rhythm of his heartbeat kept reminding me how precious life was. Especially my life with him. In his arms, I was home. "Hmmm... I'd change nothing."

22

The Ancient Ones

Max

There they were, having dinner at the restaurant on Deck 10. I did box-breathe for a few moments before approaching their table.

"My Great One, Milady."

"Ah, this youngling. Have you changed your mind about not having any requests for an exchange?"

"That one hasn't changed. Would you mind if I spoke to Milady?"

He turned his face towards his wife. "My love?"

"Hmm, his face looks serious. Don't you think so, my love? He isn't flirting with me, is he?"

"Please have a seat if it's a serious matter."

I pulled out a chair from their table. "I appreciate this opportunity."

"Ah, it is a serious matter, then," he said.

"I don't know how to start. Uh..."

"You start *umm-ing* just like your wife. You can't be overthinking while on projects, you see."

"I'm aware of that, Milady. Well, I read some stuff about you."

"Which one? There are plenty of them. Some are true, but some aren't. The Archive Department might start having headaches keeping track of those tales. If your wife starts having a headache, you know why."

"Actually, it's about her. I know I shouldn't talk about it this soon, but I've talked to my wife before deciding to come here and—"

"Ah, that one." She put down her glass of wine. "She's pregnant, isn't she?"

"Yes, Milady. She's about five weeks now."

"We do have OBGYN here. She needs to monitor your wife and baby closely. Especially once you're deployed."

"We visited the doctor last week. And we appreciate that you specifically employ female OBGYNs."

"If I were you, I wouldn't let any man touch my wife. Let alone pay him after he's done doing his job. Not in hell or earth, I'd let that happen."

"Awh, my overly possessive husband. You're rather sweet sometimes. But we need to plan another of our honeymoons for when she approaches the due date."

"I was hesitant to come here because this place is yours after all. You've been helping us so much. It didn't sit well for us to ask for more. Not to mention, this is outside of work stuff."

"That is nonsense. It's important to take care of what matters to everyone here and their families. Speaking of which, I should be thanking you for slapping my husband in the face."

"Milady?" I turned my face towards her husband and back to her.

"You know, for reminding him that anyone deployed needs to have a sound mind and not worry about their families while being away."

"You are so much in trouble, Saint. She'll be boasting about this for a long time. To provide you with some context here, this started at the beginning of our partnership. My wife insisted on cooking lunch for everyone at the smithy."

"And it turned out that I was right, my love. Loyalty needs to be nurtured. Starts from their stomachs."

I massaged my forehead as I couldn't hold my laughter. "Pffft, so that's how you keep cooking and baking for us. And that's why my wife keeps looking up the internet to search for Mexican recipes."

"How do you think my husband and I have been married since ancient times? I'd simply shove more food into his mouth. It's practical to keep him from arguing with me."

The Angel of Death and I were looking at each other, but not a single word came out of our mouths. We wouldn't even dare to breathe out any sound in response.

Mandy was in the bathroom when I came home. Throwing up and sobbing at the same time. I held her hair up from falling into the toilet bowl.

After helping her to clean up, I carried her out to sit on the couch. By holding her, I tried to soothe her as much as I could.

"Max, I'm scared. I've been vomiting up so much."

"I'm here, princess, with you. We go through this together, yes?"

"Alright." She snuggled deeper into me. "Um, I cooked steamed chicken and broth for tea. Do you want to eat now?"

"Let me ask first." I pulled her t-shirt up, exposing her lower abdomen.

"Hey kiddo, Mami cooked steamed chicken and broth. Can we eat now without throwing up again? You and Mami need to eat right." I made a light fist bump to her belly.

Looking at her, I said, "Okay. Kiddo agreed not to throw up. I'll help you eat."

23

Ascension

Max

Mandy made me feel so proud of her; I felt honored to be her husband. She was promoted to the research team in the Archive Department. And she got it while growing our baby in her.

I couldn't wait for us to pass the first trimester next week. It kind of hurt to see her struggling to even have a decent meal. She was still working in the library for resources and references she needed for her research.

Although I still needed to work on my way to say 'I love you' to her, there was nothing I cherished more than our small family. She had been regrowing my soul every day.

As for our work, we were still walking through my probationary period. By helping the more established shadow-workers prepare their projects, I got them ready for deployment. My job was similar to when I was in the Army, but now I needed to do it in a more classy and subtle way.

They told me that my movement was still too abrupt. I was still in physical and combat training, and that training was in suits instead of the uniforms that I used to wear. If anyone thought combat training in uniforms was tough enough, well, imagine me doing all of that in a suit, tie, and Oxford shoes.

The biggest difference was the technology. This institution had way more advanced technology than any government in the world, I guessed. No wonder they had been proposing the institution to help them achieve their missions. I could tell that most of the projects were governments' off-the-books stuff.

The Great One was hands-on with these trainings and briefings. He was summoning them to regroup and retrain the shadow-workers and crews as many as he could withdraw from the field. I was lucky to join this institution right after the situation in Australia.

All of a sudden, the Great One left the briefing table to walk towards the window. He opened the curtain and the window in the briefing room. Everyone in the room went silent as we watched him stare outside.

He placed his hand on his heart and said, "Oh, Divine One, please embrace her in your compassion. Keep her innocent soul in the best place in Heaven. There's another daughter of a man who ascended years ago. That flower might become a nice sister for this one. They both knew the same man."

"*Wait, was he... praying?*"

He gave a bow to the sky he kept staring at. "A baby daughter has ascended. She wasn't mine to take."

Not once did I ever think he would pray, based on what I read about him. But that made sense if he mentioned a child. I bet even nonbelievers would pay some respect to the lost innocents.

He let down his hand from his heart. He sighed heavily before turning his face towards me. "Max, your wife."

It felt like my soul had just left my body. I ran out of the room as fast as I could to the library. "*Please save my wife. Please.*"

The library's floor was covered in blood when I got there. "Medical center," said Sofia.

The elevators would be too long to reach Deck 1. So, I took the stairs to go 10 levels down. I needed to be with her more than anything now.

"*I can't lose my princess, too. Please save my wife.*"

I heard her devastating cry when I reached the medical center. "I'm here, princess."

"Max..." She showed me her bloody hands. Then her shaking hands touched her belly and showed her thighs covered in blood. "Hhh... Max."

I hugged her in my arms while the doctor and nurse were doing whatever they were doing that I didn't understand. "Shh... I got you. Eyes on me, princess. Stay with me." I kept hugging her, keeping her from shattering apart. I continued kissing her, glueing her pieces together.

The doctor tapped my shoulder and asked me to follow her to the corner. "We lost the baby, I know. The Great One knew right away," I said.

"Sir, we need to do the procedure. We need your permission to—"

"Save my wife. Do it." I left her to return to Mandy.

"Listen to me, princess. I need you to stay alive. Don't think. Just do as I say." I watched her nod. "Stay alive, and then come home to me."

Kissing her as many times as possible was the only thing I could do before they took her to the other room. The nurse gave me the papers on a clipboard for me to sign. I tried to read them, but my focus was nothing other than her safety.

On a chair in the corner, I waited for her. Close enough to the operation room but far enough from everyone. I rested my forearms on my lap, hands clasped. Shutting down, I heard no one. Staring at the emptiness, I saw no one around as they disappeared.

A caring hand separated my hands from clasping. Milady put a cup in between them. "Chamomile tea, for you." She gripped my arm and rubbed it a few times before she left.

24

My Fall

Max

With her two long strokes rubbing my face, I opened my eyes to her beauty. "Good morning, princess. How was your sleep?"

Her tears started to pool in her beautiful gray eyes. "Max, I'm sorry."

I hugged her immediately and kissed her lips. "Nothing is your fault. If anyone tries to say otherwise, they can come and fight me." My heart was shattered to have her in regret like this.

She hugged me tightly, sobbing. After a while, she said, "Thank you for being here with me. I didn't feel I deserved you."

"Where else would I be? But I need to go to the briefings this morning, though. I'll come here at noon. I need to make sure my princess is eating her lunch."

"You've been working hard. I'm very proud of you."

Before going to the briefing, I took a shower in our suite. The running water helped cool my head down a little bit. Enough to keep me going this morning.

It was the silence when I entered the room that made me want to punch anyone in the face. "I cannot believe this youngling," said the Great One when he entered the briefing room.

From the door, he opened the glass door on the other side of the room. His wings were spread out majestically. Not once in my life had I ever seen any walking being with wings. "Saint! You're no longer working for the Army."

"I'm aware of that, our Great One."

He approached me and held me by the neck. "Since you insisted on joining the briefing, let me brief you with some lessons." He pushed me, making me walk backwards towards the open glass door. He held the belt on my waist, and within seconds, we were flying up in the sky.

"Let it out, Max!"

"What—"

"I said.let.it.out, Máximo!" He released me to fall from a high altitude. No parachute, no safety net, no nothing.

I was screaming my lungs out while falling. It felt like years of screaming out everything that felt heavy in my chest. Until he caught me by the leg.

He landed us in the open area on the far Aft. Once I stood back up, he put his hands on my shoulders. "You have three days off starting today. Among all the living beings on earth, I'm the one you should listen to. I've buried enough of them since ancient times. None of our babies stood a chance to survive."

"I didn't know how to fix her. With Lani, that was why I didn't return right away when she passed. Now with my daughter gone... And with Mandy, I don't know how to fix her."

"Amongst everyone on earth, she'll be needing you the most. She needs to see you feel your feelings. She deserves to see you grieving. Man up, youngling! Fix yourself. You can't lose her, too. Take good care of your wife."

He was right that I was so used to burying myself in work back then. And he was right that I was needed at home. I was a stray dog who found my home—her. Keeping her head down, she was staring at her breakfast.

"I should help you with that."

Her eyes lit up when she saw me coming. She embraced me immediately. "Max? Shouldn't you be working?"

"I should be here with you. Otherwise, the food will be rotten, waiting for you to blink." I started feeding her slowly and kissed her each time she swallowed her food.

"Um, I miss sleeping with my blanket in our bed." Every time she called me her blanket, she made that adorable face, complete with her lips pouting.

"I miss my sleeping bolster, too. Just until the doctor says you can go."

A few days later, she was released from the medical center. The doctor required her to have a weekly check. We decided to let our daughter go into the ocean. The moment we let go, my tears started to burst out. Not even when my parents or Lani passed did I let out any tears. I buried them inside me deep enough. This time, it was Mandy who embraced me, keeping me from falling apart.

Many of them paid their respects by sending flowers to the ocean. Our Great One was right about Floret being a nice sister for our daughter up there.

Mandy joined cooking classes during her three weeks off. Since Milady knew the struggles of losing children, I figured it was the best way for Mandy to be around her.

25

Picking Up the Pieces

Max

"Good morning." She woke me up with lots of kisses and a tight hug. "You need to wake up."

I let her watch me peek into my boxer briefs. My morning wood was giving his princess a salute. "Yup, we're up. Now, where's my breakfast?"

"On the table. Come on, I've made something for you."

My hand was reaching for her pussy, sliding underneath her panties. "Ah, yes, I can feel my breakfast serving."

"Excuse me, Sir. I'm talking about an actual breakfast."

"That 'Sir' you said just told me otherwise. I want this one first. I don't mind a second breakfast."

Having the scent of her filling my nose in the morning was what I needed to start my day. Lapping her folds in the morning had become my perfect breakfast. And I wouldn't change this habit. Hearing her raw moans got my heartbeat racing.

"Oh, I've missed you inside me. Please."

"I came to the OBGYN alone. She said that I should let you decide. Besides, I like you begging." Gently, I gave her myself.

"I'm not fragile. I don't need you to treat me differently."

"Yes, you are, princess. You shatter for me easily. That's how fragile you are." That was what I needed from her. To be vulnerable around me. And what I needed from me was to praise this beautiful princess while she was surrendering herself to me. "Let me feel how much you've missed me."

I held her tighter while her wall clenched for when she came. As much as I wanted to keep it slow and steady, I couldn't hold myself back. My thrust became harder. I just missed her so much.

"Be free with me. Please don't hold yourself back."

"You should be careful with what you say. What you beg is what I give you." She begged for what she deserved. Let her have all of me inside of her.

"Du bist mir wichtig."

"You're important to me, too, princess." I watched her gasp. "What?"

"You understood when I talked with Mina? You didn't respond. But this whole time, you've listened to us?"

"Yeah, I listened when you complained about me following you everywhere. But I'll continue to follow my wife everywhere you go. No worries, I'm hard to get rid of."

"Oh, Max. I feel awful."

I poured kisses on her face. "Nah, I need to keep surprising my princess. This one gets bored easily, no?"

"Keep surprising me. I like that."

"Yes, Ma'am."

"Although I found out you also speak Russian from Kolya, remember the man helping me with my CV?"

"You tell me if he starts flirting with my wife. I'll shove him into those bookshelves."

"Owh, I have a jeallie husband. No need to be jealous. He was only giving me hints about you. There's so much I don't know about you still, Max, if that's even your real name."

"Máximo Verbena."

"That's a sacred flower. Wait, isn't that an Italian name?"

"How do you know all this?"

"Because we have some people named Verbena in Indonesia."

"Really? I didn't know that. Papi was from Argentina. There are many Italian descendants there, I guess... Well, I dunno for sure. We sound a bit different and mixed. Not sure where the name came from, though."

"Ugh, I've been listening to Castellano videos. And now I need to listen to the Argentinian accent."

"Wait, what? When did you?"

"Oh, come on, I don't always work all the time in the library. Don't tell anyone. I can't have them sack me."

"Okay, hear me out. Maybe you can learn *neutro* first. You know, the neutral Spanish. And then gradually, you learn different accents and dialects."

"How do you sound naturally?"

"Rioplatense, but I sound more Mexican for work. Back then, it was easier to blend in with my unit."

"I see. Now, I have a new mission to trace your origin. You have to see their archive, Max. They're massive." She paused to kiss me. "And your second surname, Sir? Please tell me it's Sánchez."

"Sánchez, indeed. Mami was from Mexico. My records got wiped clean when I was deep in the special forces. I chose Saint. I think they'll keep calling me Saint here."

"I've been suspicious if Max Saint is your real name. So I did some research for variations and meanings. My first bet is on Sánchez. That means the descendants of the Saintly ones, yes?"

"Ooo, I have an intelligent wife here. Gotta be careful, 'cause she smart. Haha."

26

Ways of Grieving

Mandy

"I don't know if it's the right way to make it," I said when he got out of the bathroom.

"Ay, *princesa*... I'm gonna lose these six packs." He scooped it up with the tortilla. "Mmh, I dig this any day."

"Do you like it?"

"Are you kidding me? I love it. But I love you more." He thanked me with his kisses. "It tastes like Abuella's, though."

"Excuse me. Did you just say I taste like an old woman when you kiss me?"

"Haha, not you, though some of us call our wives 'Vieja.' Literally, it means 'old woman.' But it's not in a bad way."

He scooped up some for me. "Open up." It was his way of taking care of me. And I always loved how he fed me.

"Abuella made chilaquiles like this. Mami's was different. She made it with whatever she got for that day."

"Milady taught us in the class. Maybe because she's ancient, she knows the original recipe." I prepared cutlery, but we simply used more and more tortillas to scoop them up.

He woke me up with two gentle, long strokes in my hand. "I can't read your mind, but I know you're somewhere else. Stay with me, princess."

"Um, Max. Can I ask about Lani? I wasn't that good at handling mum's suicide. This time, I want to stay, um, I mean, with you. I don't want to go out like mum."

"Oh, princess, come here." He tapped his lap for me to sit on. "I can't thank you enough for choosing to stay. Let alone, with me? Of course, you can ask."

"What was she like? How did she live her life? I want to know how she made you happy. You know, there's a chance that she'd recognise, um, our baby for looking like you."

He gave me another kiss. "First off, I have a thing with bookworms. I see a pattern between you two. Tracing things down from one book to another. Yup, I find it hot as fuck."

"But I have access to the internet; she didn't. Oh, wait, how old is she supposed to be by now? Was she younger or older than you?"

"She was two years younger than me. She should be 34 this year."

"Sir, you.do.not.look like thirty six."

"Ooo, this is your way of asking about my age? Ay, ay, ay, this woman. Well, I used to work in a library as a janitor, not like you. I met her there."

"What about her? What did she do for work?"

"She was a pilot. She told me that she needed to take off and land against the wind. Sometimes, when my unit faced, let's say, more intense challenges, it helped me a lot to keep going. Even now, working here, I keep hearing her words."

The way I smiled while staring at him might annoy him. "What?"

"I heard some of them saying that you were hard to breach. I didn't know what it meant. Now I understand why. I think I need to remember her words, too." Cupping his face with my clean hand, I kissed his lips. "Tell me more. Where did you two live?"

"We rented a house. Not big, but enough. By the time she got her terminal diagnosis, we asked her brother to help her move. She wanted to go back to Wales."

"Oh, come on. Could she not be more perfect?"

"I don't think perfection exists. Why? Did I miss anything here?"

"Welsh has a cool flag with a red dragon on it. Welsh is quite similar to people from Asian countries in seeing dragons, though. Most of us from Asian cultures don't always see dragons as evil in our folklore."

"Yeah, she told me that, too."

"I'm imagining her in my head. She was speaking with a sing-songy dialect, yes? Not like the way I speak."

"That's right. Before I met her, I thought all Brits spoke in the same way as in the news."

"No, we have hundreds of dialects."

He paused for a while. "I was grounded at home when my parents got into the accident. Fifteen at that time. I was on deployment when Lani died. It may seem like I'm good at this, but not really. I'm only well-trained to keep my shit together. And I'm sorry for your losses. Your mother, our baby."

"Max, don't say that. It's your loss, too. It's *our* baby. Not mine, ours."

"Lani was around your age when she was gone. It scared the shit outta me when you jumped, and I was terrified when we lost our baby."

"Max, please don't cry. My hands are spicy, so I can't wipe off your tears."

"Mhh, haha. No, I'm laughing now. You're annoyingly funny sometimes. My hands are spicy, too. No crying, princess."

27

Back to Barrack

Max

After we finished our probationary period, we decided to visit her mother's grave in England. Then we visited Lani's grave and her family house in Wales. I hadn't seen them for years.

We had one off-duty rotation to spend on the ground. After that, Mandy and I were assigned to the same rotation. The difference was the place we went. Mandy was boarding Slava, and I was to go to the place I used to live.

A few days before I went back, we had a meeting with the Sergeant Major. We discussed the upcoming project thoroughly, along with the limitations. Not once had I had any idea about joint projects. Probably because it was above my pay grade anyway.

This base looked different from what I remembered. It used to be named something else. It became Liberty, just as I was liberated by Mandy coming into my life.

It had only been less than two years since the last time I stepped foot on this ground. Those times made such a difference. It made me wonder how many of them were still in.

With two other shadow-workers behind me, I walked into the hall. Honestly, it was nice to see familiar faces. That way, I knew who I was going to work with on this project. But it was funny to see the room suddenly go into silence.

I looked at them one by one. "You don't need my permission to speak freely."

"Looking good in those suits, Shirt. No feeling hot in there?"

"It certainly feels good to be alive, Morales. Did you just say I'm hot? I won't tell my wife you said that. She might be jealous."

"Damn. Gone for less than two years, getting tied up already," said Johnson.

"Oh, I do the tying." We embraced each other. I didn't let him go for a while. My arms were holding his neck and body tighter. He tried to release himself and fight me back. "Told you that you need to get leaner. Johnson too big to flex?"

"Fuck, I thought you were lethal back then."

"Suit's lighter." I was in between fighting Johnson and Morales. Another shadow-worker joined us.

"What do we call you now? Suits?"

"Nah. 'Suits' are for the feds."

Eventually, all three of us danced with them in the hall. That was the start of our joint training. In uniforms or in suits, they started calling me by the name Saint. No rank, no sir, no nothing.

Twenty four shadow-workers in total participated in the ten weeks joint training. Mostly, we did combat training and classes. The thing was that they stayed wearing their uniforms, and we stayed wearing our suits.

I was used to doing the training in my old uniforms and gear. But doing all that in suits every day was something new for me. It wasn't the heat that bothered me. It was the sweat under these bulletproof suits that started to lock in under the skin. That itched the hell out of me.

At night, we lived in a place nearby that belonged to the institution. All this time, the place was under my nose. It looked like a regular big house.

They prepared a safe house for us, also nearby. But I didn't expect to be staying in that place anytime soon. What I expected was for the training to be completed so I could come home to my wife.

While on the ground, I didn't forget to buy her a gift. She deserved this gift when I came home. I imagined how good she would look with it.

28

Fishing Day

Mandy

It was time for him to come home, so I switched my day off to be on fishing day. When I saw him being fished out of the sea, I waved at him. He waved me back but went straight to the medical centre to be examined by the doctor.

Before noon, I returned to our suite and cooked lunch for him. After that, I took a shower and prepared myself for him. I picked the bra with a front hook to make it easier for him to take off. Laced black knickers would be appropriate.

While sitting on my knees, facing the bedroom door, I heard him enter our suite. I hoped that he'd like the surprises that I had for him. He mentioned them when we first made love, but I hadn't gotten the chance to get them.

"Welcome home, Sir." In front of him, I knelt. It would be easier for him to kiss me.

He held my chin up with his hand. "Nice to come home to this."

"How was your project?"

"It's completed. How is my pet doing? Hmm?" He combed my hair with his fingers, then held the back of my head with his hand.

"Missing my blanket badly." While rubbing his forearm, I said, "Lunch is ready for you."

"What if I want my dessert first?"

"No, Sir. You need to eat first."

He pulled my hair down to stretch my neck. "Ten weeks away, and you turned into a brat now?"

"I want you to have lunch first. I'm hungry, too."

I left him without saying anything. After preparing our lunch on the table, I sat on my knees in front of his seat.

"Since you're giving me the attitude, this is what you deserve." He put a black leather collar around my neck. The leash was hooked to my collar. He strapped the other end of it to his belt. He ate his lunch and fed me in between his bites while I kept sitting on the floor. With this leash, I was on all fours and following him wherever he went. To the kitchenette when he washed the dishes. To the bathroom when he freshened up.

He unhooked my leash and said, "You can use the bathroom. I'll wait on the couch. You don't walk."

After cleaning myself, I walked towards him. Intentionally refusing to follow his order. He was watching my every move until I sat in front of him. My leash was hooked to my collar once again.

"Sir, I took out the birth control last week when I was in my period."

"You don't get any reward for being a brat." He pulled the leash and collided our lips together. "I told you not to walk. How many weeks have I been away?"

"Ten weeks."

He pulled me and bent me over his lap. "Count." His spanks landed on my arse cheeks in turns. After the sixth, he removed me from his lap.

I was lying on my stomach on the wooden coffee table. Waiting patiently for him to take off his belt. No one had ever used a belt on me. "Um, I've never—"

"Well, you should've thought about that before giving me the attitude. Continue the count. Or I'll start over." His left hand massaged my cheek before each strike. He used the belt with his right hand.

"Sir, mmh... eight." My tears started to run down my face. "Nine. I've got some surprises for you. Ten."

He pulled me by the hair away from the coffee table. "Yeah? What kind?"

"I got them from a female piercer the day I boarded. I'm sure they're healed by now. Under my bra."

He unhooked the clip and pulled the cups to the sides. "So beautiful." He licked his lips while inspecting my nipple piercings. "Did it hurt?"

"I don't mind hurting for you. Do you like them?"

His mouth lapped my nipples hungrily in turn. His bites threw me into pleasurable pain. "Oh, you listened to me after all."

"Yes, I listened. There's another one, just like you told me."

He raised his face from my breast. "You really are desperate for my attention, aren't you?"

"Without question. Please, I'm drenched down there. The piece keeps rubbing me since I had it."

He laid me on the sofa. "I'll get you new ones," said Max after ripping off my knickers. He licked me along the slit with so much hunger in his eyes. He consumed my pussy with his starving mouth.

I started to move my hips, stroking into his mouth. Holding his head still. He looked so good in that suit.

"Oh, you're trying to fuck my mouth like a slut." He gave me two fingers inside me. The hole that had been empty for months without him filling it. His thumb started circling around my vertical hood. "Then come for me like a good slut."

I was clinging to his tie and shirt when he moved up. My lips parted when his fingers stroked harder. As a desperate whimper flew out of my lips, I kept looking at him straight in the eyes. To him, I let myself go.

"That's my princess. Undone. Finishing the old life she knew. Rebirthing into a new life as my queen."

Background Stories

"You cannot be a pilot and suicidal at the same time. I hope you choose to continue to be a pilot."

—Nanda Esalawati.

***

This book can be read as a standalone. This book is also a hybrid sequel, as the second book in **The Ark of the Shadow-Workers: A Collection of Legend, Myth, and Folklore Retelling** and the third book in **Max Saint: A Fictional Biography**. Since the authors in the collection write for different audiences and genres, we publish the story in separate books.

The book *Growing Her Wings: A Romantic Novel for Aspiring Pilots* is an inspirational story that focusses on how Leilani and Máximo support each other in pursuing their careers of choice. The book is written by a pilot, providing the industry's insights through clean and wholesome fiction for young adult readers.

The origin story of Máximo Verbena Sánchez goes from the moment he met Lani until they both established their careers. The passing of Lani has never been mentioned in that book. The tragedy has not been told until the book *Sky Flower: Romantic Stories for the Ones Who Are Left Behind.*

Princess Mandy in this book is inspired by a Southeast Asian folktale. By the time this book is published, ironically, the folktale of Princess Mandalika (or Mandalike) is still being published as a children's book, even with the depiction of a suicide. The folktale is still circulating in the origin country and being exposed to minors.

In the original folktale, she was receiving two marriage proposals from two princes from different regions. To prevent the war between two kingdoms and her own, she decided not to choose either of them. She said that she would pronounce the winner of her heart. Then she invited the two princes to come to a place one morning, so they would have a better view to watch her jump off the cliff. The seaworms were believed to be the reincarnation of the princess.

The authors of the books, along with the publisher, felt the need to give the princess a chance to survive. With the help of Max Saint, she could make her rebirth into a more fulfilling life.

About the Author

Rada Lyubomirova retells the myths, legends, and folktales with a darker taste and morally grey characters. Each story is to reimagine childhood stories in either historical or contemporary literary art. Her works are to give rebirth to the timeless narratives that have enthralled generations.

Her writing style is a tasteful blend of dark romance with a medium-to-fast burn rate. Classic stories are given a seductively darker twist to guide you with a passion that will keep you delightfully hooked deep into the night.

As the author enjoys her travel time, her books invite you to take an enchanting journey through exotic lands to return to treasured childhood memories. By meeting people from different cultural backgrounds, the author finds that myths, legends, and folktales may unite people.

Through exploring foreign lands, the author sees the commonalities that connect cultures through stories. She finds it fascinating how these tales travel across borders and unite people in a sense of wonder and value to pass down to the next generation.

Rada cherishes the bond and collaboration she has with her readers. Your feedback shapes and enhances the realms she creates in the literary arts. Is there another tale, legend, or folktale that has fascinated you? Leave your thoughts and reviews on her stories.

About the Publisher

Besides publishing fiction and non-fiction books, Compendia Publishing creates content for social media and online courses.

Scan the QR code above to see our portfolio of work.

***

Thank you for purchasing the original copy of this book.

Your feedback will help both the author and the publisher with future works.